NEWCOMER
in New Albany

by
Phil Hardwick

QUAIL RIDGE PRESS
Brandon, Mississippi

Other books in Phil Hardwick's Mississippi Mysteries Series:

Found in Flora
Justice in Jackson
Captured in Canton
Vengeance in Vicksburg
Collision in Columbia
Conspiracy in Corinth

To be included on the Mississippi Mysteries mailing list, please send your name and complete mailing address to:

QUAIL RIDGE PRESS
P. O. Box 123 • Brandon, MS 39043
1-800-343-1583

DEDICATION

This one is dedicated to the
most unique citizen of New Albany.
You know who you are.

ACKNOWLEDGMENTS

Many people in New Albany helped make this book possible. At the top of the list is the Board of Directors of Main Street New Albany, a committed group of individuals who care about New Albany's downtown and its history. Special thanks go to Billy Wiseman, who is a patient, guiding community leader.

Thanks also to the many people who shared their memories, opinions, and news about life in New Albany today and yesterday. To those who made the author's visits a pleasant experience, much thanks is given.

Chapter 1

It did not look good for the Ole Miss Rebels. Although they had possession of the football, only two minutes and twelve seconds remained for them to upset the highly favored Buckeyes of Ohio State University in a game agreed to a decade earlier by two athletic directors who had long since moved on to other career interests.

A national television audience and a capacity crowd at Vaught-Hemingway Stadium looked down on a green field drenched by a late September sun. Many television viewers had already switched to the Notre Dame vs. Michigan State game. Nevertheless, no one here at the home field of the Rebels had abandoned his seat, hope being the elixir of the underdog.

The Rebel quarterback glanced up at the scoreboard and considered the situation. The opponents led by ten points, 24 - 14. It would take at least two scores to win the game. As he brought his team out of the huddle and to the line of scrimmage, I felt the pressure tighten on my right arm. My companion's hands were squeezing it tightly. We stood and yelled with tens of thousands of others. The crescendo grew louder. There was still time, if only Ole Miss could score soon.

At the snap of the ball from the center, the quarterback dropped straight back, as an onslaught of three Buckeye front linemen, collectively weighing over a thousand pounds, overpowered the Rebel offensive line and bore down on their intended victim. At the last possible second, the quarterback heaved the ball high into the air toward the goal line forty-five yards away. It wobbled its way upward in a high arc and began its descent toward an end zone of grass painted red and blue. As the football fell through an altitude of ten feet above the ground, a red-jerseyed receiver streaked across the goal line, snatched the ball from its flight, and ran full speed through the end zone; the striped-shirted referee raised both arms skyward to signal a touchdown.

The multitude instantly erupted in cheer and jubilation. Laura, my girlfriend, Ole Miss Law School alumnae and rabid Ole Miss football fan, leaped toward me, threw her arms around my neck and screamed, "Did you see it! Did you see it!" It was an exclamation, not a question. I wondered if my middle-aged, one hundred eighty-eight-pound frame could withstand her celebration.

"Yes. Yes, I saw it," I replied, pleading for mercy.

"They're going for two," she said, exhaling. She took a deep breath. "They are going for two," she exhaled. "Oh, my God. I can't watch," she said, lowering her head and peeking out from her hands simultaneously.

The Rebels lined up for an attempt at a two-point conversion. Success meant there would be only a two-point difference. A field goal could then win the game.

A one-point conversion could produce a tie, at best. Although a field goal would still be necessary, this play meant the Rebels were going for a win, not a tie.

The quarterback surveyed the Buckeye defense, saw something that he didn't like, and changed the play at the line of scrimmage, yelling out to his backfield and line. At the snap of the ball, the offensive and defensive lines melded into a mass, the quarterback took one step backward and fired a bullet of a pass to a wide open tight end in the end zone. The score stood at 24 - 22, with exactly two minutes left to play. Laura went completely berserk, jumping straight up and down and yelling, "Yes!" repeatedly.

Ole Miss kicked off to the Buckeye team, which then slowly and methodically marched fifty yards down the field from their own twenty yard line, where the ball had been spotted after the kickoff had gone into the end zone. With every gain of yardage, the volume level of "dee-fense" cheers fell lower. The temperature on the field of play was almost ninety degrees, and obviously the heat and the Ohio State offense were taking their toll on the home team.

The Buckeyes now had the Rebels right where they wanted them. A man sitting at my left shoulder muttered something to the effect that at least the effort had been valiant. Laura squeezed my right arm even harder and said hopefully, "It's not over yet." Of course, I knew otherwise.

With eighteen seconds left on the game clock and first down at the Ole Miss thirty yard line, the OSU quarterback did the unthinkable—he heaved a pass to his right, toward his flanker. Normally, such a pass is safe, but one does not throw any kind of pass when all it takes is three snaps to run out the clock. The play would be debated for weeks by Ohio State fanatics, and some would allege that big money had been involved. But none of that changed the moment, for just as the ball was thrown, the Ole Miss defensive cornerback raced forward, snatched the ball from high in the air before it got to the Ohio State flanker, bobbled it for a second and began to gather it in. Tens of thousands inhaled in that instant. Then a loud roar went up from the stands. As the player brought the prize down, it slipped under his shoulder and fell to the ground, an incomplete pass.

The Ohio State coach sent in the second string quarterback who followed his instructions to a tee and ran out the clock without ever letting the ball be handled by anyone other than himself and the center. The final score remained at Ohio State 24, Mississippi 22.

Laura and I slowly made our way to the parking lot, hearing the term "if only" at least a half-dozen times. It had been a great game. It had also been a great day. We started it out with a hearty breakfast at the Olde Tyme Deli in Jackson, then drove three hours to the University of Mississippi campus in Oxford. She's a big-time lawyer at a powerful firm in Mississippi's capital city, but acts like a college preppie when we return to football games at her graduate school alma mater. I enjoy these trips, but not with the same level of enthusiasm as my "significant other." My college days were at night, taking courses in criminal justice while working full time as a cop in St. Louis, Missouri. Now retired after twenty years of service, I live in my boyhood home of Jackson, Mississippi, and supplement my retirement income doing work as a private investigator.

Work was blending with play on this trip. Yesterday I had received a call from a middle-aged man who identified himself as Kadley Sturgis, owner of a radio station in New Albany. He had a shallow, almost feminine voice. He explained that the station went on the air for the first time this past Monday morning. That afternoon saw the Mississippi debut of Jill Polaris, "the brightest star on radio." She was on the air from three o'clock p.m. to six o'clock p.m. doing the thing that many talk show hosts do—stirring up the listeners. Apparently, the listeners were shaken, not stirred, as James Bond would say, because Jill Polaris did not report for work the next day and had not been seen or heard from since. There was no sign of foul play, so all that the local police could do was take a missing person's report and broadcast a bulletin. The station owner did not buy it. He felt that she had been kidnapped.

I asked him why he thought that. In a breathless voice that sounded as if he needed more air, he said that to understand I would need to hear the tapes—the tapes of Jill's show last Monday. If I would just listen to the tapes, I would see why someone would want her off the air. He wanted to drive to Jackson and deliver them personally. I assured him that was not necessary. I ultimately agreed to pick them up in Oxford after the football game.

"Where are you supposed to pick up the tapes?" asked Laura, as we approached her new Jaguar XJS, resting regally in the parking lot. I had briefed her about the call during the drive up from Jackson.

"He said that they would be at the front desk of the new Hampton Inn out on Highway 6. I'm to pick up a package and open it in the parking lot." I looked at her with a sheepish grin. "Don't suppose you want me to drive back?"

"Not a chance," she said, opening the driver's door. "Remember our agreement."

How could I forget? She had allowed me to drive her new masterpiece to the game and she would drive home. It was pure driving satisfaction to be behind the wheel of the Jag.

Traffic was still heavy as we drove out of the campus and onto the highway. Soon, however, we were pulling into the parking lot of the motel. I got out and went inside. Behind the counter was a young woman in her early twenties wearing a smart-looking vest and pants outfit.

"Hi. Do you have a package for Jack Boulder?"
I asked.

"I surely do," she said with a smile. She stepped into a small office to her right and emerged with a large manila envelope. My name was on the front in black permanent ink from a felt tip marker. There was no return address.

"Do you happen to know when this was left here or who might have left it?" I probed.

"Sorry," she said with a smile. "It was here when I got here."

I thanked her, got back into the Jag and opened the envelope. Inside I found two standard-size cassette tapes, a brown manila envelope with the name "Jack" printed on it and a sealed, white, business-sized envelope, which I opened immediately and read.

Dear Mr. Boulder:

Thank you for agreeing to review the matter we discussed on the telephone. Enclosed are last Monday's tapes of the Jill Polaris show. They should give you plenty of insight and reveal the cause of my suspicion. She did not show up for work on Tuesday, or any day since. I fear that she may be in trouble. I wish to employ your services to find out what has happened to her. Enclosed is a retainer. Please call me after you have listened to the tapes.

K. Sturgis

Attached to the letter was a cashier's check for $2,500. I handed the letter to Laura and asked what she thought.

"I'd say you have got a serious client," she replied.

"Looks like I might be spending some time in New Albany."

Chapter 2

The two standard-size, ninety-minute cassette tapes each had an orange label. The first label read, "Jill Polaris, Monday, 9-22, 1-A." The back side was 1-B and the other tape was labeled similarly with sides 2-A and 2-B. I inserted the tape into the Jaguar's sound system and leaned back in the passenger seat as Laura drove south on Interstate 55.

"Good afternoon, New Albany. I'm Jill Polaris and you and I are going to make history today." Surprisingly it was a soft, bedroom voice. I had expected the staccato of a shock jock. "This is the day when New Albany gets its very own public forum, a place where people like you can say whatever is on your mind about politics, lifestyles, what you like and what you don't like—you name it. You can even talk about what goes on behind closed doors—both the public ones and the private ones. And all you powers-that-be, you are forewarned. This medium is for everybody. So pick up the telephone and give me a call. I'll be waiting. And I'll be back right after this message."

There was a commercial. Actually it was a public service announcement informing battered and abused women that help was only an 800-number away. Then the calls came in. Most were local citizens welcoming Jill Polaris to New Albany. One caller wanted to talk about the political antics of the Speaker of the United

States House of Representatives.

We continued south on Interstate 55 while listening. Although the tapes were of a show that was almost a week old, it was as if we were listening to live, call-in radio. If pressed to do so, I would categorize the first hour of calls as welcome to New Albany. The second hour transitioned into a discussion of politics. Jill Polaris was far less controversial than I had anticipated. Most talk show hosts, whether on radio or television, seem to thrive on the arguable. She was empathetic with most callers. For that reason it was easy to see how the third hour saw a change of tone. Practically all of the callers were women. The theme of the last hour drifted toward the subject of relationships. Soon, women from all over north Mississippi were sharing deep secrets about their boyfriends and husbands. One caller did not especially appreciate the program.

"Jill, you should know that the woman who called before me tends to—shall we say—be a little casual with the truth," said a nasal-sounding caller who identified herself as Wanda.

"Are you implying that she is a liar?" said the still soft-spoken voice from Jill Polaris.

"Well, I didn't say that exactly, but you know what I mean."

"How is your relationship with your husband, Wanda?"

"Not bad," replied the caller. "It's the lying women

who are going to call you that make me mad. You should get ready for that. Of course, some of us know how to deal with lying women," said Wanda snootily.

"How is that?"

"We just take them to a place they can't lie any more." The caller now sounded as if her teeth were clenched. I would bet that her hand was made into a fist. "And some of them never come back."

"Where is that place, Wanda?"

"That is for me to know and for you to find out," she lashed her enraged reply.

"You're suddenly not very comfortable talking to me, are you, Wanda?" This Jill Polaris was one cool cookie who knew how to run a radio show.

"You're a liar, too," the caller yelled. "Liar, liar, pants on fire!" came the scream and then a loud click.

Jill Polaris did not miss a beat. She put the next caller on the air immediately. "Hi. You are on the air with Jill. Would you like to tell us about your relationship?"

"I suppose so," said the timid-sounding voice. "My point is that relationships change over time. Some of these callers just need to hang in there. Things really can change. They just need to have a little faith."

"How has your relationship changed?"

"It's gone from distrust to trust." The voice was no longer timid, but had become firm and more articulate. A professional woman perhaps.

"How so?" asked Jill.

"When we were first married, I didn't trust him. He was gone at weird hours and his excuses were too vague."

"So what did you do about that?"

"I hired a private detective and had him followed."

"Did you catch him doing anything he should not be doing?" asked Jill Polaris.

"No," said the caller. "I don't think he was fooling around at all."

"But you say you trust him now?" probed the talk radio host.

"Yes. We've grown to know and understand each other a whole lot."

"Well . . . thank you for calling," said Jill. "And our next caller wants to talk about a relationship with her boss. Go ahead. You are on the air with Jill."

A woman who sounded as if she were in her fifties began discussing her relationship with her boss, the manager of a local retail store. It seems that the boss was married, but that his wife "must know by now" that her husband had "a paramour." One woman was a friend. One was a lover.

"So what is your point?" queried Jill.

"I guess my point is that extramarital affairs aren't always bad."

Jill bid the caller farewell and then said, "What about it, north Mississippi? Are extramarital affairs always bad?" She paused. "I see by the clock on the wall that we have only about two minutes left, so we will save that topic of conversation until tomorrow."

She thanked the listeners for calling, said how delighted she was to be in New Albany, and then signed off. Laura and I spent the rest of the drive to Jackson discussing the subject of extramarital affairs. We agreed that they were not healthy things to do.

Chapter 3

Monday morning I rented an almost new Ford Crown Victoria for my trip to New Albany. It was the closest thing to a police-looking vehicle on the lot. There were only fifteen hundred miles on the odometer and the new car smell was a pleasant aroma in my nostrils as I pulled out of the parking lot and said a mental goodbye to my 1968 Camaro, a fully-restored beauty that was a testament to nostalgia and middle-aged craziness. I've learned that when working on cases in small towns, it helps to look the part. People there expect an investigator, even a private one, to look halfway official. I had been tempted to chose a sleek, red Mitsubishi 3000 GT for the trip. It looked like I felt.

I took Interstate 55 north and was quickly out of the capital city and into cruise control territory. I moved the seat adjustment two notches back and listened again to the tapes from last Monday's Jill Polaris Show as the rolling Mississippi countryside slipped past. Two hours and fifteen minutes later, I turned onto Highway 7, then Highway 30 over to New Albany. The land had become more hilly and covered with lush forests. There was no shortage of kudzu, the vine that grows so fast that planting instructions are to throw it over your shoulder and run.

It was lunchtime when I arrived in New Albany, so I decided to find a place to eat before paying a visit to

Kadley Sturgis at the radio station. At State Highway 30 and U.S. 78 there was the usual assortment of chain restaurants, motels and gas stations. I try to avoid chain eating establishments, opting instead for a local eatery. I like a little local flavor with my food, and chances are good that the meal in a local place didn't arrive in the back of a refrigerated eighteen-wheel tractor-trailer. Highway 30 came to a "T" intersection at Bankhead Street. I turned right, and less than a mile later, drove over a two-lane bridge and was deposited into the downtown area, a retail district of mostly two-story brick buildings. Parking spaces were arranged diagonally in front of the sidewalks on either side of the street, and few were available. This was one downtown that was not dying. After two blocks I crossed a railroad track and noticed what I suspected was the county courthouse on my right. As I continued up a mild incline, it occurred to me that New Albany was not like the typical southern county seat, where there is a square in the middle of town featuring either the county courthouse or the standard Confederate soldier statue facing south. New Albany had more the flavor of a New England town, with its Main Street, flowing stream and steepled church.

A few blocks later I spotted just the kind of hometown diner I was looking for. Its architecture was classic American roadside. Lots of tinted glass, concrete block, and aluminum awning. The name on the sign said "Jimbo's." I turned left into the parking lot, found a spot and went inside to an interior that could be just as at home in Kansas or South Carolina. It was open and functional. There was no put-on in these kinds of places. One came to eat. Regulars also came to talk. This was the type of place that has no equal for catching up on local gossip. Sure enough, over in one corner were the regulars. There are two clues to spotting such groups. First, there will be two or three tables pulled together so that there is a new larger table. Second, the group will be drinking coffee instead of eating food. When they stop to eat, they go to other tables to do that. Usually with family members or co-workers.

After a table server took my order for the blue plate special, I tuned my ear to the topic of conversation from the regulars. There were five of them. All men. Two wore neckties and business shirts, two wore plaid work shirts and one wore a polo shirt. They ranged in age from thirty-five to sixty-five.

"I hear that they are going to show the Rebels on TV this week against the Razorbacks," said one of the neckties.

"After they almost beat Ohio State, it's no wonder," said a plaid shirt.

"Rebels and Razorbacks," said the other necktie, leaning back and tilting his head upward with eyes searching overhead. "Always a close game. Used to go to every one of 'em. No need to now. Hell, you can see fifteen football games on TV every Saturday and Sunday nowadays."

The others all nodded in agreement as if some profound words of wisdom were laid on the table for contemplation. The polo shirt spoke. "I'll tell you what's gonna take over football. It's going to be soccer. Have you seen how kids are playing soccer all the time now? They are gonna have to add some soccer fields at the Sportsplex."

"That New Albany Sportsplex was one of the best investments this town ever made," said plaid shirt. "I never saw as many baseball and softball tournaments as I did this past summer."

"I heard that," said someone.

There was a long pause while each of them sipped their coffee and cleared their throats. About that time my meal was set in front of me. I knew by looking that I could not eat everything on the plate—it was overflowing with food. One of the best things about the meal was that the price was three-fourths of what one would pay in Jackson or Memphis. I began eating but stopped in the middle of a bite when I heard one of the regulars say something about "that talk radio lady." I listened more closely.

"Anyway, I hear that after last Monday's show, she decided to just leave town."

"Why would she do that?" said polo shirt. "She just moved here."

"Maybe she didn't leave of her own free will," said another voice in the group.

"That's ridiculous," said one the plaid shirts.

"I don't think so," said necktie. "My cousin at the police department said that the radio station manager filed a missing person's report, but they can't do anything so the manager's thinking about bringing in a private detective. By the way, did any of you hear the show?"

I glanced over that way. They were all shaking their heads negatively.

"It's a crazy world we live in," said one of them.

Chapter 4

After lunch I headed back downtown. The radio station was easy to find. It was right behind the courthouse and it looked like a jail building—plain and functional. I walked in and was greeted by a receptionist who couldn't have been more than twenty years old. I gave her my name and told her that I was here to see Mr. Sturgis. She invited me to have a seat, and I did so while she disappeared into a back room. It may now be a radio station, but it still looked like a jail. Obviously none of the walls had been moved. Remodeling concrete block and steel would be difficult, I suppose.

Kadley Sturgis strode out of a back room wearing a purposeful look on his face and carrying a clipboard full of papers. He took sixteen steps to cross the room to me when only eight would have worked just as well. I'd put him in his mid-fifties, dark hair with a prominent bald spot on the top rear of his head, five-foot-ten and approximately 165 pounds. He wore black rim glasses—the type that were popular in the fifties—and a white short sleeve dress shirt. A navy blue necktie and pants of the same color completed his outfit. I detected a slight stoop in his back.

"Let's go back to my office," he said with a look over my shoulder, "where we can talk."

He ushered me back to his minimally furnished office and sat behind a metal desk that was cluttered

with papers. As he sat down, he motioned me to a wooden chair directly in front of his desk.

"Thank you for coming so soon, Mr. Boulder," he said in a soft, raspy voice that sounded as if too much cigarette smoke had left its mark on his voice box. "Did you listen to the tapes?"

"I did."

"Well, what do you think?" he asked, leaning forward.

"Sounds like just another radio talk show to me," I said. "Actually it was quite tame compared to some stuff on radio today."

"You didn't hear the threat?"

"What threat?"

"The one at the end of the show."

"Why don't you tell me about Jill Polaris?"

He rolled his eyes slightly and said, "What do you want to know?"

"As much as you know," I replied. "Let's begin with

her employment history. Do you have a resumé? An employment application perhaps?"

He gave me one of those "you just don't get it" looks and exhaled a little too loudly. As if everybody knew the details except me. He was not far from correct on that point.

"Everybody in radio knows Jill Polaris," he said, opening the bottom right-hand drawer of his desk and extracting a magazine. He opened it to a page about midway through the periodical, leaned forward and laid it in front of me. It was a radio industry publication. I picked it up and was confronted with a full-page article about Jill Polaris. The gist of it was that she was one of the top five female radio talk show personalities in the country and could have been number one if only she had accepted an offer to go to New York to one of the big stations. Instead, she surprised the radio world by leaving Dallas and taking a job at a new radio station in the small Mississippi town of New Albany. Her explanation was that she wanted to get away from urban America and go to "real America." There was the stock disc jockey photo of her wearing earphones, sitting behind an oversized microphone and a control board. She was a beautiful woman, about thirty years old with golden, blonde-streaked hair worn in a ponytail. She was tanned and fit, maybe even a bodybuilder, judging by the shape of her arms. She wore an orange tee shirt and a blue jean vest.

"How did you meet Jill Polaris, or whatever her real name is?" I asked.

"Yes, that is her real name," he said settling back in his chair and folding his arms across his chest. "I met her in Dallas two years ago. She was hired from a smaller station in San Antonio. I was the sales manager. She took us to number one in less than three months. Took Dallas by storm. I had been trying to get my own station for a long time, which is a hard thing to do these days. In short, I heard about this license for a new station in New Albany, wound up buying it and moving here. When I told Jill about it, she asked me if she could come, too. I almost fell out of my tree. Like the article said, she was looking for a small town. It was the luckiest thing that ever happened to me. I even had plans to syndicate her show nationwide."

"And now she's missing," I said.

"And I want you to find her," he countered. "She's worth a lot to me. I'm willing to spare no expense."

"Any ideas?"

"My best guess is that it's some local yokel," he said. "Yesterday's show may have been too threatening for north Mississippi."

We talked for thirty more minutes and he gave me the details of what he knew about Jill's move to New Albany. She had arrived on the Thursday before her first Monday workday, driving across the Tallahatchie River bridge into downtown in her new Corvette. She checked into the Heritage House, a bed and breakfast on Main Street, and let it be known that she was in the market for an older home, preferably antebellum. She showed up for work as scheduled at ten o'clock a.m. Monday and seemed excited about her new radio home. She had spent most of the weekend riding around town, checking out the local scenery. Tuesday she failed to appear and no one has seen her since Monday night at the Heritage House.

"What about Dallas?" I asked. "Have you checked back there?"

"I thought about that, too. I've called there every day and nobody's heard from her."

"Who have you called?"

"The radio station and her landlord. Here, I'll give you the numbers," he said, and handed me a piece of paper with the radio station and apartment numbers.

"Did she have a boyfriend in Dallas?"

"No. She was totally into her work."

At that point, I decided to change the subject. Looking at the ceiling, I said, "This is an interesting building."

"Yes. It was the county jail. They were going to demolish it, but it was sold to private interests who wanted to preserve it. The second floor still has all of the cells in place. It turned out to be a great layout for radio equipment up there."

"Could I take a look? I'm an old police officer who

has seen a jail or two."

He uncrossed his arms and said, "I'm afraid that will not be possible. It must be maintained as a secure area." He stood up and walked around to the side of his desk. It was his way of saying that our conversation was over. "Where are you staying?"

"Where was it you said that Jill Polaris stayed?" I asked.

"The Heritage House. It's about two blocks from here on Main Street," he said, gesturing a direction toward the front of the building.

"I'll stop by and see if they have a room available, and will report to you tomorrow or the next day."

Chapter 5

The Heritage House was located at 307 Main Street, two blocks up from the radio station. Main Street in New Albany is not the main street in the traditional sense. The main street in New Albany is really Bankhead Street, which is one block north of the real Main Street. This part of Main Street is a residential street, rich in turn-of-the century to mid-century homes with established yards of flowers and fully grown trees. The house was built in 1911 and has eighteen rooms within its five thousand square feet of living area. There are six bedrooms available for guests. The living room and double parlors feature exposed beams and twelve-foot ceilings. Hardwood floors are found throughout the house, and in the parlors and dining room is an inlaid pattern believed to have come from Italy. There is also a glassed-in side porch for guests who like their breakfasts in the morning sunlight. Heritage House sits above street grade and invites visitors up the concrete steps to its large, wraparound porch. I accepted the invitation.

As I reached the top step, I heard a squeaking sound and looked to my right to find a dark-haired, middle-aged woman gently gliding back and forth on the porch swing. She dragged her foot to stop the swing and came forth to greet me. She introduced herself as the manager, Deborah Taylor. I told her that I needed a room for maybe two nights. She escorted me back to a library, where I completed a reservation form.

"I only have one room left for tonight," she said pleasantly. "It's ten dollars more, but it's the suite."

"I'll take it."

She gave me a tour of the downstairs, then took me up to my room. It was located on the right front of the house and had a sunroom attached to the high-ceilinged bedroom. The sunroom had two walls of floor-to-ceiling windows and was furnished with a sofa, two chairs, and a small roll-top desk. In the corner was a single bookstand containing a television/videocassette recorder combination, several hardbound novels and a dozen video tapes of recent movies. The bedroom had a dark green wall, a small fireplace, a four-poster bed that one crawled up to get into, and a chaise. On the night table was a Tiffany-style lamp and two books. As Ms. Taylor bid me a good evening, I picked up one of the books and discovered that it was a work entitled *La Tulipe Noire,* by Alexandre Dumas. It was printed in French. I must confess that in my night classes while working on my degree in criminal justice, I was not exposed to very much French or Alexandre Dumas. I set his book down and picked up the other. It was a book of love poems written in English. I could read this book, but I was in no mood for love poems. An action video was more of what I had in mind for this evening.

I went to the sunroom and pulled a recent Sean

Connery movie from the selection in the bookstand. I inserted it into the VCR, turned off the overhead light, and turned on a lamp. I removed my walking shoes, propped my feet on the coffee table and settled back on the small sofa. I picked up the television's remote control device, aimed it at the TV and pressed the "power" button. At that instant there was a knock on the bathroom door. At first I thought it was a noise from the television. After all, how often does one hear a knock from the bathroom door? I opened it with a mixture of curiosity and trepidation. Upon doing so I felt that I had been transformed back to the sixties and one of those shampoo commercials. Standing in front of me was as stunning a woman as I had ever seen. She had blond, shoulder-length hair, a perfect smile, pert nose and an aura of—well—happiness. She was barefoot and wore tight blue jeans and a man's blue oxford, button-down dress shirt, tied in a knot in front so that much of her firm stomach showed.

"Hi," she smiled even wider and stuck out her hand. "I'm Ellie. Welcome to New Albany."

"Thank you," I said, not taking her up on the handshake offer. My built-in warning system was sending me messages that something was not right here. "How did you get in my bathroom?"

"This door," she said, stepping back and revealing a door to her right. "It leads to my bedroom. Looks like we have something in common."

"What's that?" I asked.

"Our bathroom," she said with that smile again. She stepped past me into the sunroom. She looked as good from behind as she did from the front. My male libido began intruding on my warning system. She spun around on one foot and said, "And what might your name be?"

"Jack Boulder," I replied, sticking out my right hand.

Shaking it firmly she said, "You must be that private investigator they brought in to find Jill Polaris?"

"How would you know that?"

"New Albany is a small town. Word travels fast."

I deduced that whomever this goddess might be, she was probably a good source for a lead or two. I invited her to have a seat on the sofa. She did so, assuming a position with legs crossed in a modified yoga position. I clicked off the television and sat in the rocker.

"Did you meet Jill Polaris?" I asked.

"Of course. She stayed in the bedroom across the hall. She moved in a week ago Thursday and did not come back Tuesday."

"Is her stuff still here?"

"I don't think so," she answered. "Deborah said that Jill's boss came by and picked it up Wednesday."

"What about her car?"

"It hasn't been seen since Monday evening," she said.

"So tell me about you," I probed, a grin making its appearance on my face.

"I grew up in New Albany. Our family moved to Ohio when I was a sophomore in high school. Went to college at Ohio State—did you know that Ole Miss almost beat them last week?" she said with a squeal.

I started to tell her that I was at the game, but doing so would only interrupt her monologue. I was here to listen.

"Anyway, my grandmother got sick, so I'm spending a month with her. She's in a nursing home. They say that it's very important that she be visited by a family member every day or she will forget her family. It is a sad case."

"What kind of work do you do?"

"I'm a computer programmer. I can log on to my job

and work via the terminal. My company has no problem at all with that."

This was one modern woman. She had an up-to-date flexible kind of job, looked like a model and was intelligent. I thought that it would be nice to have dinner with her. But first I needed to extract more information.

"So what was Jill Polaris like?" I asked.

"Tell you what," she said, standing up and clasping her hands behind her back. "You buy dinner at the Village Café and I'll tell you all about Jill Polaris."

Chapter 6

Eleanor "Ellie" Saline and I walked from Heritage House to downtown, passing by the radio station and crossing diagonally across the front lawn of the Union County Courthouse, a structure built in 1909 and listed on the National Register of Historic Places. We strolled by the New Albany Police Department, an interesting art deco building itself.

Our four-block walk took us to the heart of downtown and home of the Village Café and Java Stop. It had, as they say, atmosphere. Exposed brick walls were adorned with giant black and white prints of people like Paul McCartney, Elvis Presley, and, of course, William Faulkner. The black tin ceiling gave the place a spacious feeling. The ceiling fans swirled the aroma of coffee beans and oven-baked foods. This was no greasy spoon. I would bet that it would be hard to even find grease in the kitchen. We placed our orders and settled back into our chairs.

"This is an interesting place," I remarked. "Not exactly what I expected in a small town."

"I don't know what you expected, but New Albany is not your typical small Mississippi town." She leaned forward. "To be sure it's got its share of small town attributes. Like most places, only a few people have most of the real power. And like most places, there has been an occasional scandal or two."

I took a sip of my iced tea and prodded, "Give me an example."

She laughed, tossed her hair back with a flip of her head and said, "One of my favorites is about the rich, well-established man whose illegitimate son showed up after he died. It seems the man—I will not mention any names—had been fooling around with one of the women in a sharecropper family on a farm outside town. Apparently the man had lived all of his married life with this little secret and no one ever knew. While the lawyer was probating the estate, in walks this seventy-some-thing-year-old man and announces that he is the son of the rich man."

"Was he?" I asked.

"Apparently so," she said with a smile. "He had

some type of proof, and he got the money. Unfortunately, he had lived most of his life by then."

"You know a lot about New Albany for someone who only lived here until tenth grade."

"My mother is a history teacher. She made sure that I knew everything there was to know about this town. I haven't forgotten. Besides, I would always come back in the summers and visit my grandmother."

"Tell me another New Albany story," I said.

Before she could begin, our server appeared and convinced us of the merits of having a cappuccino and biscotti for dessert. It did not take much persuasion for either of us. Moving to the table next to us, she made the same pitch to a couple who had just finished dinner. We did not pay any attention until the server mentioned the radio station.

"Oh, Veronica," said the server to the woman at the table. "I loved your call to the Jill Polaris Show last Monday."

"I beg your pardon," said the diner nervously.

"Yes." It was a little too loud and too nasal, I thought. "I can't believe you had ole Lamar followed by a private eye." The couple went wide-eyed, and more than one head turned toward their table. The server winked at the woman and said, "But I'm glad you trust him now. We wouldn't know what to do without Lamar around here."

As the server walked away, Lamar grimaced and

looked directly into his wife's eyes as if cross-examining a child molester, and in a voice that could be heard clearly for fifteen feet around him said, "You did what?"

The wife remained calm. She picked up the napkin from her lap and dabbed her lips before speaking. "Ten years ago, I thought you were running around on me, so I had you followed by a private detective one weekend."

His eyes grew large, and his whole face took on a wild look. He pushed his chair back from the table, rising as he did so. Suddenly he slammed both hands on the top of the table with a force that sent the salt and pepper shakers two inches in the air and overturned a glass of water. The words spewed from his mouth.

"You go straight to hell!" he said loudly and stormed out of the restaurant.

Chapter 7

Later, Ellie and I walked back toward the Heritage House under a three-quarter September moon, in night air that was beginning to feel cool. Autumn does not usually come to Mississippi until October or November. However, a hint of it slips in once or twice in September. A weather front will move through, causing rain, then the next day or two will be cool and sunny with a clear, blue sky five miles high. Within a couple of days, the haze and heat return along with the knowledge that autumn was simply teasing.

Another sign of the coming season is the discernible change in the color of the leaves. The sycamores will even let go of some of their postcard-size leaves to float down and be blown around. That was exactly what was happening as Ellie and I strolled across the courthouse lawn.

After the incident in the café, we had not said much to each other, joining other patrons in awkward silence. We stopped walking and took a seat on a wooden park bench. I was the first to speak.

"Did you know that couple back there?"

"I just know who they are," she said. "He is a hot-shot attorney; she is an interior designer. They were made for each other. Both are over-achieving yuppies," she said. "I remember him from school. We are about the same age."

"And what would that be?" I dared to ask.

"The big three-oh," she said unoffended.

"What are their names?"

"He is Lamar Crafton, local despicable plaintiff attorney who only takes the cases involving defendants who have good insurance. I talked to him once about suing another nursing home where my grandmother was staying for improper care. He said they didn't have enough insurance for him to fool with it. You ought to see his advertisement in the telephone book. It is obscene." She paused a minute to settle down, then continued. "The wife is Veronica Crafton, interior designer. She has a shop on Main Street in the same block as the Village Café. It's never open, though. She doesn't cater to people in New Albany. She goes to homes and offices in Oxford and Tupelo and Memphis. Her nose stays up in the air a lot."

I sensed that there was some reason for her animosity, but decided not to press the issue. The last thing I wanted was for her to get riled up.

"Before we were interrupted back there, you were telling me some local interest stories," I said. "Would you care to continue?"

She leaned forward and went on to tell me one of the most interesting stories I have ever heard. It seems that in the early 1900s, an heir to a large fortune in a northern state decided to move to New Albany. He was a man who had a passion for hunting and the outdoors.

He purchased thousands of acres of land nearby and built an estate that would have fit in well in Newport, Rhode Island. The property included an octagonal-shaped barn made of brick. The main house had fine tapestries and the best of furnishings. There was even an indoor pool. All of this in an area where many houses did not even have running water at the time. He threw elaborate parties. Guests came by rail from the northeastern United States and stayed overnight at an exquisite downtown hotel he had built just for that purpose. Besides the parties, there were fox hunts and polo matches.

The man allegedly had a girlfriend who stayed at the estate. She is said to have loved poodles so much that she owned a dozen of them. They even slept in the same room with her, and when she got cold at night, she just added another poodle to her bed. To protect the poodles from getting wet when they needed to go outside during the rain, an addition with a dirt floor was added on to the estate house.

This millionaire was a frequent visitor to the continent of Africa, where he hunted with international outdoorsmen of all types. It is said that he was the first American to be granted a license to use dogs to hunt lions. It is also said that during a trip by steamer across the Atlantic, he was told by a spiritual man of some kind from India that he would die before he reached his next birthday. The prediction was immediately scoffed at.

That very night, his companion—the one who loved poodles—learned that he had found a paramour during the trip. He died later that night from unknown causes. A favorite rumor is that his girlfriend poisoned him, saying that if she could not have him, then no other woman could have him. The next day was his birthday. He was later buried at sea.

"That is quite a story," I said. "Are the estate and the hotel still intact?"

"Both burned down a long time ago," she replied. "However, I understand that there was a railroad stop near the place and that there is a grave site there maintained to this day."

"While we were eating, you said that William Faulkner had a connection with New Albany."

"Of course. He was born here," she announced. I bet her mother would have been proud. "His father was the railway agent here at the time of birth. He only lived here one year of his life, then his family moved to Oxford after his father received a promotion. Do you read much Faulkner?"

"I'm more a reader of crime novels and techno-thrillers. I did read *The Bear* once. That's a great story," I said. "By the way, is the birthplace still standing?" I asked.

"Nope. Long gone. But there is a sign. Would you care to see it?"

"Sure," I replied, and we leaped up from the park

bench and headed what I judged to be northeast. About four blocks later we were standing at the corner of Jefferson Avenue and Cleveland Street, home to a historical marker noting the significance of the place.

William Faulkner
Here, September 25, 1897, was born the distinguished author, member of the American Academy of Arts and Letters, winner of the Pulitzer Prize and recipient of the 1949 Nobel Prize in Literature.

I looked around and considered the current land use. A red brick church now resided on the site. Directly across the street was a lovely white house complete with full-width front porch, white picket fence and an aura that said it was a prime candidate for a *Southern Living* feature story.

"Let's get back to Heritage House," she said, and to my surprise, grabbed my hand, interlocking our fingers. We walked back to the bed and breakfast holding hands like high school sweethearts.

Chapter 8

Upon arrival at Heritage House, we went upstairs to the sunroom and sat down together on the small sofa. On the coffee table in front of us was a small crystal bowl of chocolate-covered strawberries. From a compact disc player against one of the walls, the love songs of Julio Iglesias filled the room.

"We talked a lot tonight," she said as she began gently running her fingers through my hair. "You cleverly avoided letting the conversation get around to you. Now it's time for you to tell me about Jack Boulder."

"It's short and sweet," I said. "Andrew Jackson Boulder is a retired St. Louis homicide detective. I live in a downtown Jackson condo that overlooks Smith Park, which is basically between the Governor's Mansion and the State Capitol. What else? Oh, I jog five mornings a week to maintain my one hundred eighty-eight pounds. And I'm divorced with no kids."

"Do you have a girlfriend?"

I knew this was coming. Being a male, there was a part of me that wanted to go there. There was another part of me that was screaming out caution.

"Yes. One girlfriend," I said.

"Marriage ahead?"

"No. We like it just the way it is."

She placed her other hand on the inside of my leg. I am a grown man who has been around the block a few times, but right then I was feeling like a seventeen-year-old on a date with the prom queen. My legs were like jelly.

"Let me be very direct," she said, moving her hands and clasping them in her lap. "I want you—physically, I mean." I felt a lump forming in my throat as she continued. "There are two kinds of men—those who will, shall we say, have an encounter with another woman, and those who won't. Those who will, believe that one can give to another, and nothing will be taken from the first relationship. Those who won't, believe that it does take away from the first relationship. Which type are you, Jack?"

I looked into her eyes, and then at her nose, her lips and her chin. She was without a doubt one of the most desirable women I'd ever met. Was she testing me? Was this a game to see which way I would answer? I leaned forward and kissed her lips, holding her face in my hands. It was a long, lingering kiss, the kind that is a prelude to other pleasures. Then I leaned back and looked into her eyes again—gorgeous eyes.

"I'm sorry," I said. "I guess I'm the kind that believes something is taken away."

"Then why did you kiss me? Are you saying that you don't want me?"

"Physically, I want you more than anything right now," I replied. "But I just can't do that to my girl-friend. I know what I would do if I saw her in this position with another man."

She stood up abruptly, walked over and jerked open the bathroom door—the one that connected to her room. She turned and spit the words. "You just made a big mistake, mister."

Chapter 9

The next morning I paid a visit to the New Albany Police Department, which was located on West Bankhead Street about midway between the Union County Courthouse and City Hall. There were two reasons for making contact with local authorities. First, I wanted them to know what I was up to. They could make my life miserable if they chose to do so. I was an outsider moving in on their turf. Sometimes that had consequences. Second, the local police department could be a good source of information. As always, there was probably information that I needed to know.

I pulled open a heavy door bearing a government seal with an American Indian on it and went inside. After identifying myself to an officer behind the counter, I was led back to the office of Sgt. Perkins, who was the day shift commander according to the sign on his door.

Perkins would have made a good model for a police recruiting poster. He was about six feet tall with dark hair cut in short, military style. In his late twenties, the flat abdomen and shaped biceps proclaimed his excellent physical condition.

I introduced myself as a private investigator and told him that I had been hired to search for Jill Polaris. Still standing behind his desk, he asked how he could be of assistance.

"No way, really," I said. "I just wanted to let you know I was in town and what I was doing."

"Have a seat," he said, pointing to a wooden chair beside me. "You are aware that we have taken a missing person's report and put out a lookout for her?"

"I am."

"She's an adult, you know."

"I know."

"If she were a juvenile, we could put out a lookout with much wider coverage," he said. "We could even put it on television and radio."

"I understand."

"But she's an adult," he repeated. "And there is no evidence of foul play. We do what we can under the circumstances."

I raised my hands in the surrender position and said, "Hey, Sergeant. Nobody is saying that the police department here is not doing all that it can do." I let my hands back down.

"Where did you say you were from?" he asked. "Memphis?"

"No. Jackson."

"Your name is awfully familiar," he said. "What did you do before you were a private eye?"

"I spent twenty years with the St. Louis Police Department."

"That's it," he declared with a snap of his fingers. "We reviewed your case last year in a criminal justice course I took at the community college. You're the cop who shot the guy who killed your partner. You got him coming in for arraignment. That's you, isn't it?"

Here we go again. I was never going to be able to live down the incident in St. Louis. "It is," I said rather softly, remembering the nationally publicized trial. My partner, his wife and daughter had been killed during a burglary of their home. When the dirt bag who slaughtered them was captured, he just mocked the system. He said that he was glad to have wasted a cop. He was out on parole for armed robbery at the time and had a rap sheet several pages long.

Sergeant Perkins stood up. I just sat there, wondering if he was going to throw me out or lock me up. He was suddenly animated. He moved from around the desk and came toward me.

"Let me shake your hand," he said as he grabbed my right hand. "The professor had our class do a mock trial on your case. We all voted to acquit you. Just like the real jury did. The professor wanted to convict you, but what does he know? He's an academic." He took a step back and grinned. "It's a pleasure to meet you, Mr. Boulder."

Chapter 10

Thanking him, I walked outside, then into the offices of Crafton and McVee, Attorneys at Law. A redheaded receptionist working busily at a word processor greeted me.

"I'd like to see Mr. Crafton," I said.

"Did you have an appointment?"

"Not exactly."

A man appeared in a doorway to one of the back offices. He was every bit of six-feet-four inches tall and had a thick head of light brown hair. He had the beginnings of a pot belly and wore a pair of dark, elastic waistband slacks, a white shirt and a red tie that hung loose around his unbuttoned shirt collar. I guessed his age at fifty-five.

"I'm his partner. Maybe I can help you," he said, leaning against the frame of the doorway, arms folded across his chest.

I stuck out my hand and introduced myself as a private investigator from Jackson working on the Jill Polaris case.

"Jill Polaris, huh?"

"That's right," I replied.

"I'm James Lee McVee. Come back into my office," he said, taking one step back. I walked in. He closed the door behind me.

The office was smaller than I had anticipated. The

oak paneling did little to enhance its size. There was one entire wall of bookshelves. I noticed that there were no law books on the shelves, just books about lawyers and how to manage a law office. Behind his cheap-looking desk was a set of three double-hung windows that looked out over the side lawn of the courthouse. He sat in a black leather judge's chair, plopped his elbows on the desk, and just looked at me.

"Well, go ahead," he grunted.

"Actually I'm looking for your partner, Mr. Crafton," I said, attempting to break the ice and get him talking.

"He'll be back in a week."

"Maybe I should come back," I said, starting to rise.

"Maybe you should tell me what you're after."

"Of course," I said, leaning back in my chair. "Last night Mr. Crafton had a small scene with his wife at the café after he learned that she had called in to the Jill Polaris show Monday. He told her where she could go and then he stormed out."

"Lamar did that?"

"He did."

McVee began laughing, then guffawing and finally, coughing. His secretary rushed in with a glass of water and he composed himself. His character completely changed. He now seemed jovial and friendly.

"That damn Lamar," he said, still laughing. "I bet he doesn't come back from Alaska."

"I beg your pardon," I said.

"Lamar Crafton is on a plane to Alaska as we speak. My guess is that he is somewhere between Chicago and Seattle right now. From Seattle, he will fly to Anchorage and from there take a small bush plane to some remote site where he will spend the next five days hunting bear and elk and whatever else happens to roam through his gun sight. It's his annual ritual. He will be totally and completely out of touch."

"So he should be back next week?"

"Wednesday, to be exact," he said. He leaned back and snickered, then turning to me said, "Tell me exactly what happened."

I gave him an account of the events of last evening, pointing out how abruptly and angrily Crafton had left the restaurant. He seemed to be very entertained by this. I decided to be direct.

"What is so funny about all of this?" I asked.

"Boulder, let me let you in on something that may explain a few things. Lamar went to Ole Miss—undergraduate and law school. He played football. He was the big man on campus, as they used to say. He could have any woman he wanted. They were all after him. And you know which one he chose?"

"Something tells me it wasn't his wife."

"Hell no," he guffawed. "It was Jill Polaris. They were a big item for two years over there. Everybody thought Jill and Lamar would get married right after graduation. But he went to law school. She told him she couldn't wait on him anymore. Boy, was she stuck on him."

"Do you know if they kept in touch after school?"

"Not that I know of," he said. "Lamar came in here and joined the firm right after law school. That was about six years ago. By the way, that Crafton name on the firm was his father. Edgar Crafton passed away about three years ago. Lamar seems to be happy here."

"Will he stay?"

"I suppose so," he replied. "He seems to like it here." There was a pause. "When he's here."

"Is he gone a lot?"

"You have to be gone a lot when you do what he does," he said, turning to gaze out the window behind him. "Lamar is what some people call an ambulance chaser. He's a plaintiff's lawyer. Loves to sue big corporations with good insurance who take advantage of poor little Mississippians. He's already made over a million dollars in legal fees. It took me ten years to do that."

"Would his father be proud of him?" I asked.

McVee turned and addressed me. "Edgar would be rolling over in his grave if he knew some of the stuff Lamar was doing. Edgar—Lamar's father and my former law partner—was as fine a man and lawyer as ever lived. He would cringe at the thought of his son advertising legal services. He considered it a disgrace to the profession. Have a look at Lamar's latest gimmick."

He reached under his desk and pulled up a red bumper sticker with white letters that read "BACK OFF—My Lawyer Is Lamar Crafton." He shook his head back and forth.

"No other lawyers around town like Lamar because he is so pushy. But they all envy him because he's going out and making money. Do you know how many cases he has tried in three years?"

"Probably not very many," I said, knowing what the answer was going to be.

"None. Not one," he said. "He sues, then settles. He wouldn't know how to practice law."

"So what made him the way he is?" I asked.

"Fate," he replied. "Pure damn fate. Lamar began his career wanting to help the poor man. You would not believe the indigent people who came into this office that Lamar helped with getting their social security or some money or benefit owed them. One day a man with no leg came in. He had it cut off by a train when he was laid out drunk on a railroad track. Lamar was negotiating with the railroad, but wasn't having much luck. About that time Lamar went to a course on insurance claims and learned how to make them pay. He filed his lawsuit in a south Mississippi county known for giving judgments against railroads. He settled for half a million. His cut was 40 percent. He had found the gold mine."

"You think he will go back to being what he was

once he makes a lot of money?"

"How much is that? He's already made a million and that's not enough. No, it's not money that will make Lamar's life complete."

"What do you think it will take?"

"Probably something that you are looking for," he said.

He looked at his watch and reached for his jacket. "I gotta go. I'm in court in two minutes. Call me later if you want to talk some more."

Chapter 11

My case was finally starting to take shape. At least I had finally found someone who might have some semblance of a motive for wanting to get rid of Jill Polaris. I needed to know if Veronica Crafton knew that her husband dated Jill Polaris in college. There were several ways to find that out. All of them except one involved extra time. I decided to go right to the source.

I headed straight down to Veronica's shop, mentally planning my questions as I walked along. Suddenly a man stepped out of an alley directly into my path. I stopped just in time and moved quickly into a crouched position. He was coming right at me now from my front. He stopped six inches from my nose.

He was somewhere between forty and seventy. It was difficult to tell because he was slightly stooped, wore coveralls and a heavy dark green cardigan sweater with a white band around the collar. He sported a four-day old scruffy beard and had stains of smokeless tobacco juice dried on his chin. He looked like he had slept in the same clothes for several nights. His eyes were squinted as if the sun bothered them. Clutched in his hands was an AM/FM radio/cassette player. A cord connected it to small headphones over his ears.

"Wait!" he said to me loudly. "You wanna hear my song?"

"What?"

"You wanna hear my song? I wrote it and they are playing it on the radio right now," he said gesturing to his ears. He took off the headphones and thrust them to my chest. "Listen. They're playing my song."

I put one of the small speakers to my ear. It was grimy and moist. I heard nothing.

"Yeah," I said, handing it back to him. "That's really good."

"I wrote that. I'm Alfred." He walked around me and headed on down the block, saying "Yeah, I wrote that and they are playing it on the radio."

I wasted no time in getting over to Veronica's shop. As I crossed the center of Bankhead Street, I noticed something that I had not seen before. Cars were parked in two lanes in the center of the street as well as diagonally against the curb. It was as if the double yellow line did not exist. Perhaps only retired cops notice things like that. Then again, it was now almost ten o'clock, when shoppers would be downtown.

At Veronica's shop, the "closed" sign had been flipped over and the "open" sign was displayed. I walked into the vacant but lighted showroom. Veronica came strolling out of the back office and stiffened up when she saw me.

"May I help you, sir?" she asked in a businesslike tone.

"Perhaps you can," I replied. "My name is Jack Boulder. I'm investigating the disappearance of Jill

Polaris, the radio talk show host."

"I'm afraid I know nothing about the matter," she retorted.

"But I think you do, Mrs. Crafton. Could you tell me where your husband is?"

"You're the investigator—you tell me!" she exclaimed.

"Perhaps you'd like to tell me about your husband's relationship with Jill Polaris."

"I'm sure I don't know what you are talking about," she said.

"Fine. Let me explain it to you, then. Your husband left suddenly last night when he found out you had him followed. Presumably, he left to go on his annual hunting trip to Alaska this morning. I might mention that your husband and Jill Polaris used to be lovers, but you already knew that."

The last sentence had its intended effect.

"Jill Polaris is a home-wrecking whore," she said firmly, but in conversational volume. "She came to New Albany for one purpose—to steal my husband. Well, I've got news for her—she's not going to get him. And I would appreciate it if you would just go on back to Jackson and leave well enough alone up here."

"Did you talk to Jill Polaris face to face, Ms. Crafton?"

"The door is behind you, sir. Please don't let it hit you on the way out."

I turned and walked out the door. It occurred to me that living with this woman might be as bad as spending time in that radio station when it was the old jail.

I paused for a moment and studied the people walking up and down the street, living their lives, minding their own business. The disappearance of Jill Polaris did not seem to have caused much of a stir. Life went on. I watched the front door of the Village Café open and release a young man and woman holding hands. Ellie and I had held hands while walking the night before. She probably wanted to see me leave New Albany, too. The couple stopped for a moment and studied the window display of a bookstore then went into Sappington's, an upscale clothing store.

Wait a minute. Couples hand-in-hand. Leaving New Albany. Why didn't I think of it before? The incident at the café could have been a ruse. Trip to Alaska. Buy a week's time. Was it possible that this whole thing was a setup so that Jill Polaris and Lamar Crafton could leave town together?

Chapter 12

The first thing I needed to do was find out if Lamar Crafton went to Alaska and, if so, whether he traveled alone or with a companion. That would be easier said than done. I couldn't just call up airlines and ask if he had boarded a plane to Anchorage. Maybe the legal secretary could help. I walked briskly back to the Crafton and McVee law firm. She was still working on the computer.

"Hi," I said cheerfully. "Did James make it back from the courthouse yet? I was supposed to get some information from him."

"No," she replied. "He could be there all day. Perhaps I can help you."

"I'll bet you can. He was going to get me Lamar's itinerary—his flight times for his Alaska trip."

"Oh, I have that right here," she said opening a desk drawer. "Let me make you a copy."

Within a minute she had done so, and I was on my way back to the Heritage House to pack my bags. I was checking out and heading to Memphis where Lamar Crafton would have caught his flight this morning. If luck was with me, I would find out if he had gotten on that flight. If not, then I had another plan up my sleeve.

As I walked by the radio station, it occurred to me that it would be ethical and proper to keep my client informed of my activities and discoveries. I went inside, asked to see Kadley Sturgis and was immediately ushered back to his office. Even the activity of a radio station could not disguise the heart and soul of this building—a jailhouse.

I walked toward Sturgis, who remained sitting behind his desk, and told him about the events of last night at the café and my interviews this morning. He smiled and nodded his head affirmatively.

"Excellent," he said.

"I'm going to drive to Memphis and see what I can find out at the airport. I'll call you or come by when I have something to report."

"Can I interest you in lunch? There is a diner right around the corner that has a hamburger so good, people eat it for breakfast. It's a real experience. A trip back to the good old days."

"Maybe next time," I said. "I need to get to Memphis."

I walked out of the radio station and headed up Main Street toward my place of lodging. The summer heat had returned and brought with it the humidity. I could feel my polo shirt sticking to my skin already. Two short blocks later, as I was approaching the Heritage House, an old man on a front porch across the street waved at me. The house was a bungalow style, its porch containing four wooden posts on top of brick bases. He was sitting in a cane rocking chair, going back and forth. Hard work and persistence solve cases. Although I was in a hurry, I decided to pay a short visit to the elderly gentleman.

"Kind of hot today," I said walking up his front walkway.

"Just right," he said with a grin on his lips and a twinkle in his eye.

I introduced myself and told him why I was in town. He nodded as if he knew that already.

"I wonder if I could ask you a question?" I said.

"Go right ahead, young man."

"Do you spend much time out here on the porch?"

"Just from sunup until sundown," he answered.

"Did you happen to see that radio lady leave for work last Tuesday morning?" I asked. "The one they call Jill Polaris."

"Yep. Saw her Monday and Tuesday mornings."

"Tell me what you saw," I said gently, trying to hide my excitement over what sounded like a new lead. This was the first time I knew of anyone seeing her Tuesday.

"Well," he began slowly, "Monday morning she came walking down those steps about nine forty-five and walked to the radio station."

I looked across the street to the Heritage House and two blocks toward the radio station. It was possible to see her all the way to the station.

"The next morning she came out early. About the same time you did when you went jogging this morning," he continued. This old guy didn't miss a thing. I certainly didn't notice him this morning. He would make a good witness. "Only that morning she got into that sports car of hers with that other young woman that's been staying over there, and drove off. And that is the last I've seen of her."

"Do you know the name of that other woman?" I asked.

"I think they call her Ellie Mae, like on the Beverly Hillbillies—no, I believe it's just Ellie."

"Did you see them return?"

"The one they call Ellie came walking back at about nine o'clock that morning. Haven't seen the radio lady, though."

So Ellie had been with Jill Tuesday morning. I distinctly remember her telling me that she last saw Jill Monday evening. Was it just a mistake or was Ellie somehow involved?

Chapter 13

I checked out of the Heritage House shortly after noon. Ellie was nowhere in sight. Ms. Taylor said that she had gone to visit her grandmother. An hour and fifteen minutes later I was in the parking lot of the Memphis International Airport.

I cruised around in search of a Corvette with a Texas or Mississippi license plate parked beside a vehicle with Mississippi plates from Union County. I had no luck finding the Corvette, but I did discover a Jeep Grand Cherokee with the Mississippi plate I was looking for. There was something else that gave me a clue as to the owner's identity. On the back bumper was a big red sticker with white letters. It read "BACK OFF—My Lawyer Is Lamar Crafton." Just to double check, I got out of my car and peered into the Jeep. There was a window envelope with Crafton's name in plain view. Apparently he had gone to Alaska.

My original plan had been to go back to Jackson, regroup, and then return to New Albany. However, I

BACK OFF
My Lawyer is Lamar Crafton

knew I would not rest until I went to Dallas and talked to Jill Polaris' old colleagues. I also realized that I knew very little about my so-called victim. Sturgis did not have a resumé and I had learned quite by accident that she went to college at Ole Miss. She could have grown up in New Albany, for all I know. The more I thought about it, the more foolish I felt.

Northwest Airlines had a direct flight to Dallas that left in two hours. My arrival time would be seven-fifty p.m. I bought a ticket and found a concourse deli that sold hot dogs. I ordered one with sauerkraut and the instant I bit into its biology-lab taste, I resolved to try the Chicago-style hot dog at the Village Café when I returned to New Albany.

After polishing off the dog and some chips, I meandered down to the passenger waiting area near my gate. I took a seat close to the floor-to-ceiling glass window so that I could watch the planes come and go. There wasn't much activity at this time of day and my mind started working out the permutations and combinations at play in this case. I found a writing tablet in my overnight bag and started making notes.

One—random violence. Two—intentional disappearance. Three—With L.C. on purpose. Four—With L.C., kidnapping or whatever. Five—Jill Polaris/Ellie? Six—Veronica C. Seven—Caller. Okay, that makes seven possibilities to work with. I decided to rank them. Items One and Seven were least likely, so they were at the bottom of the priority list. I somewhat liked item number two. It made the most sense. After all, here was a woman on her way up. She probably is getting anxious about how she will handle the big time. Especially New York. One way out, so to speak, is to head to a small market. She does so, but finds that she has made a big mistake. Where would she go? What would she do? It is logical that she would go right back to the security she had just come from. She would do that in her white Corvette. And that is why I was going to Dallas.

Item Three was next on my priority list. She and Lamar could have decided to run off together. I don't remember anybody saying that Lamar and Veronica had any kids, so there would be no complications in that regard. It would be fairly easy to do. Besides, that scene at the restaurant was a little overplayed, in my book. He was just a bit too intense and seemed to make sure that everybody in the restaurant witnessed the event. A lawyer would think of stuff like that.

The possibility that Lamar had taken her against her will seemed extremely improbable. Nevertheless, her coming to New Albany could have caused him some real problems if she were after him and he had no use for her. His career could have been threatened. His wife may have given him an ultimatum. But the obvious question remained—would Lamar Crafton have been better off if Jill Polaris was gone? That was a tough one. I did not need to automatically throw out the possibility that Crafton did her in.

Then there was Item Six. Veronica Crafton certainly had a motive. A former girlfriend comes to town and attempts to take away her husband, even if it is a husband she doesn't like. Veronica had the personality for it, too. I would do further investigation of Veronica Crafton.

Item Five was most troubling. Ellie had lied to me. Why? What was she hiding? What was her real relationship with Jill Polaris? Had they met before Jill checked into Heritage House? I had a lot of work ahead of me. My thoughts were interrupted by the announcement about my flight.

"Northwest Airlines announces its boarding call to Dallas. We will begin by pre-boarding . . ."

How in the world is it possible to pre-board an airplane? One is either boarded or not boarded. There were so many oxymorons in the aviation world that it's no wonder so many comedians use them for stand-up comedy routines.

Based on the large crowd in the waiting area, I figured this to be a full flight. My boarding pass only added to that unfortunate conclusion. I had a center seat on row thirty-one. Nothing like buying a ticket at the last minute. I would probably be wedged between two professional wrestlers. As the line moved forward, I finally found myself inching my way down the aisle of the cabin toward my assigned row. It took a while because every other person carried some type of overstuffed bag that had to be crammed in the overhead compartments. When I was a young man, airline travel was considered a special event. These days it has become a cattle call.

When I reached row thirty-one I discovered something other than I expected. In the window seat was a cute teenage girl wearing boots and jeans, and in the aisle seat was a woman about sixty who looked like a Sunday school teacher. Both were slim. I wedged my way in and sat in the center. The Sunday school teacher pulled out a paperback novel and began reading. The teenager grinned and said hello.

"Hi. I'm Aslea. Going to Dallas or on to somewhere else?" she asked with a pleasant grin.

"Dallas," I answered. "How about you?"

"Yep, that's home for me."

"Do you listen to radio a lot in Dallas?"

"All the time," she replied.

"Ever hear of a disc jockey named Jill Polaris?"

"Are you kidding? She's like the best thing on radio. Or maybe I should say that used to be on radio."

"What happened to her?"

"I think she moved to some small town in Mississippi," she said. "I guess she just wanted to get away from it all. But she was the best thing that ever happened to Dallas radio."

For the next fifty minutes our plane chased a setting sun and my seatmate and I talked about Dallas. She knew everything there was to know about the Dallas radio scene. I enjoyed her company. She made the flight seem like only a few minutes.

Chapter 14

Jill Polaris' former radio station was located on the north side of town in a business park at an Interstate 635 interchange. I rented a Pontiac Firebird at the airport rental facility and hit the freeway. I drove less than a mile before I encountered a toll booth that bottlenecked twelve lanes of traffic into five. I started and stopped for eight minutes that seemed like twenty. Thank goodness I found an oldies station on the radio.

After getting through the toll booth, I accelerated onto the highway with four other drivers who had floored their accelerators. What the heck. We were in a race. The posted speed limit was sixty-five, and at seventy miles per hour, I was getting left behind. I backed off , deciding that I didn't need a traffic ticket in Dallas.

I checked into a nationally franchised ten-story hotel across the street from the business center where the radio station was located. Assigned a room on the seventh floor, I was given a plastic card that made a small green light illuminate on my room door, allowing me to enter.

Before settling down, I dialed Laura's number in Jackson. For all she knew, I was still in New Albany. Her voice mail answered and I left her a message to return my call. I started thinking about what had happened last night with Ellie. One part of me was proud that I could resist and not go any further with her. Another part of me felt guilty for doing what I did. Men my age grew up in a society in which the male was considered a hero or a stud if he made it with a lot of women. Females, on the other hand, were taught that a bride who didn't walk down the aisle a virgin was somehow less than desirable. Someday the sexes may work all this out. I guess what bothered me most was that I know how I would feel if I walked into a room and found Laura being kissed by someone like I was kissing Ellie. I admit it. There is a double standard. Men really are from one planet and women from another. I didn't contemplate this issue very long, because the telephone sounded its electronic warble at me. I picked up the handset after the first ring.

"I didn't think you would call back that quickly," I answered cheerfully, expecting to hear Laura's voice. Instead it was the voice of a middle-aged man.

"Leave town, Boulder," it said maliciously. I could see his sneer through the telephone. "And do it right away or you will wind up like your car."

There was a click, indicating that he had hung up. I walked over to the window and saw an orange fireball in the parking lot. My rental car was fully engulfed in flames.

Chapter 15

The next hour was spent downstairs in the lobby talking to fire investigators and police officers. I used a pay phone to report the fire to the car rental agency.

Contemplating my next move, I knew that one thing was certain—I was being followed. Spending the night in the same room would result in no sleep because I would just lie there knowing that someone was outside my door, up to no good. It would not be a wise move to leave the hotel, either. He or they would just trail along to the next one. There was a different cashier behind the counter than had been there when I checked in. I walked up and said hello.

"Yes, sir," said the clerk in non-recognition. "May I help you?"

"Yes. Do you have any singles? One person, one night."

"Let me check," he said, tapping the keyboard on the computer beside him. "Yes. I have a room on the fourth floor. It's a nonsmoking room."

"That will be fine," I said. "I'm not much for smoking tonight."

I paid cash and registered under the name of Bob Morgan. He gave me a key-card and I found my way to the room. It was identical to the room on the seventh floor that I had been in earlier. However, no one knew I was in this room. Oops, there was a problem with that.

Laura would attempt to call me back and get no answer. I called and left another message. Only this time I told her not to call me back, that I would catch her at the office tomorrow.

Changing rooms was a good idea. I knew that. If someone tried to come after me, he would go to the wrong place and I would be safe. That is, unless I was observed checking in the second time. I realized that I was beginning to get a little paranoid. There were probably few observations of me with the police and fire around. My guess was that someone was paid to deliver a message and that it had been delivered. Nevertheless, I hardly slept that night.

The next morning I walked across the street to the objective of my visit. The radio station was on the ground floor of a mid-rise concrete and glass building. I had expected a plate glass window where passers-by could watch the deejay work. Not so. The layout was just like any other business office. The reception room had a few posters of national network radio personalities on the wall, but that was about it. The receptionist sat behind a curved counter and was accepting a package from an overnight delivery service when I walked in. She greeted me warmly and I asked to see the station manager.

"Did you have an appointment, Mr. . . . ?"

"Boulder," I said. "Jack Boulder. Here's my card."

She looked at it curiously. That was the typical reaction. The only thing on the card is my name and telephone number. No address. And no line of work. I'm not one of those who use my business card for marketing purposes. People either know about me and need my services or they don't. It's strictly word of mouth.

"May I tell him what it's in reference to?" she asked.

"Jill Polaris," I deadpanned. "I'm a private investigator."

She took my card, walked through a door behind the counter and returned in forty-five seconds.

"Mr. Royce will be right with you."

Two minutes later Mr. Garry Royce, the station manager, came out and explained that he had been on a telephone call. He ushered me back to his contemporary-designed office and invited me to sit in a chair at a small conference table. The wall was covered with certificates and plaques of all types from press organizations. He looked and dressed the part, wearing a stylish gray suit, black silk socks, expensive black loafers and a maroon tie with silver diamonds. He took off the coat, draped it over the back of the chair, and sat down.

"She said this was something about Jill," he said, worriedly. "Is she all right?"

"I'm afraid she has disappeared," I said, waiting for a reaction that did not come. "She did not report to work last Tuesday morning and hasn't been seen in New Albany since."

Then the reaction came. "Oh, my God," he said as

he inhaled a large gulp of air and placed his right hand over his mouth.

"I'm a private investigator hired to find her. I wondered if she may have come back to Dallas, or if any of her acquaintances here have had any contact with her since she left."

"Not that I know of, but I'll be glad to check. We are having a staff meeting in about an hour," he said, being as helpful as he could be.

Then he dropped a bombshell on me. "Of course, none of us could believe it when she resigned to go to New Albany. I'm sure it's a nice little town, but the fact that she went with Kadley was what surprised us."

"In what way?" I asked.

"She was afraid of Kadley Sturgis—well, not really afraid. She was leery of him. He had a serious attraction for her. He sent her flowers, presents and all sorts of gratuities, such as concert tickets and special passes to professional sporting events here in Dallas. He was always trying to get her to go out with him. There was a rumor around the station that she thought he was stalking her. It all came to a head about nine months ago when I had to fire him."

"What was he like?"

"He was a cad," said Royce. "He was not very sociable around the station. He thought others who worked here were beneath him. He didn't get along very well with most of the other employees."

"So why did you tolerate him?"

"Because he is the best sales and marketing person in radio today. He is a genius at knowing what the market wants. And better than that—he can sell advertising like nobody else. We had a waiting list of sponsors for Jill's show, and that was with a 50 percent premium added to our normal rate card. I hate to say it, but I would love to have him back for what he can sell."

"Have you talked to him since he left?"

"No," he said. "No one around here has heard from him since he left." Now there was a revelation. Sturgis had told me that he called her apartment and the radio station every day.

"Let's talk about Jill Polaris," I said.

"Jill Polaris," he repeated and became pensive. "The brightest star on radio. It was true. She was very special. She connected with the listeners and she knew about relationships."

"What about her relationships?"

"I don't know that she had any serious personal relationships," he said. He walked over to the opposite side of the room to a small wet bar and poured himself a cup of coffee without offering me one. "I just can't understand why she would go work at a station owned by Kadley Sturgis," he lamented. "There is no amount of money that would persuade her to work for him. I still don't believe it. There must be something else in New Albany that attracted her."

"There is," I said. "But it's a long story."

Thanking him for his time and information, I borrowed a telephone in a vacant adjacent office and arranged for a taxi to pick me up in front of the hotel in thirty minutes. I walked back out into the reception room and said goodbye to the receptionist. Across from her was a man dressed in a business suit sitting in a chair reading a magazine as if waiting for an appointment. He looked up from the slick, colorful pages and glanced at me in nonrecognition. But I recognized him. I had seen him Monday night in New Albany. He was Lamar Crafton, attorney at law.

Chapter 16

It was exactly twenty-three minutes later when Lamar Crafton emerged from the radio station. I had spent those moments sitting on a concrete bench by a small fountain in the shade of the building overhang.

He walked across the street to a parking lot and opened the door of a late model Buick that had a rental company sticker in the lower right corner of the rear windshield. I walked that way. When he stuck the key in the ignition I moved in and tapped on the passenger side window. He lowered the power window and as he did so I reached in and unlocked the door. I pulled it open and sat in the passenger seat facing forward.

"What are you doing? Are you crazy? Is this a car-jacking?" He was panicking. "I'll give you anything."

I slowly and deliberately turned and stared at him. I paused before saying, "Give me Jill Polaris."

"What are you talking about?"

I figured it was time to bluff. If the right words are used, lawyers are easiest to bluff. Once they know your side has the advantage, then all they want to do is plea bargain or settle.

"We can do this two ways, Mr. Crafton," I said. "We can talk here or we can go down to precinct twenty-two. The choice is yours."

"What do you want to know?"

"Why don't you start by telling me what you are

doing in Dallas?"

"Looking for Ms. Polaris," he said. "I'm a lawyer from Mississippi. She is . . . she is . . . my client . . . "

"Cut it, Crafton. You are starting out in a bad way. Why don't you just put that transmission in gear and I'll tell you which way to go."

"No! Please listen. I have to find her."

I didn't say a word. I merely stared at him. The pregnant pause. The trick that lawyers use when they have witnesses on the stand who aren't telling the complete truth. Just stare and don't say a word. Most people can't stand it. They become very uncomfortable. They must say something.

"She was supposed to meet me in Memphis," he said rather meekly.

"That is a long way from here," I said. "You missed a turn somewhere."

"You don't understand. I was supposed to meet her at the Memphis airport."

"And where were you supposed to go from there?"

He paused a long time. It seemed to me a little longer than it should. He finally said, "Chicago."

"That does not explain why you are in Dallas," I said.

"She didn't show up. She's missing. I thought she might have come back to Dallas." Suddenly he got brave. "Look. Just who the hell are you? Why should I answer your questions?"

"Because I'm a private investigator who has been hired to find Jill Polaris. And what do I find when I go looking for her but an old boyfriend who is supposed to be bear hunting in Alaska." I said, using the same note on each syllable. "Now that makes you a suspect, I'd say. And I believe that the Dallas police, or better yet, the FBI, might like to hear your little story."

"Okay, okay," he said, raising his hands to the surrender position. "You got me, but it's not what you think."

"So what is it?"

"Jill's an old girlfriend," he said. "A week or so ago she shows up in New Albany and tells me she's moving back. She said she was going to be a talk show host at that new radio station. We spent most of the weekend together and decided that there may still be a flame flickering there. We planned to go to Chicago and spend some time together."

"You mean run away together, don't you?"

"That is one way of putting it," he said.

"And the final destination?"

"New York," he said. "She had an incredible job offer there. I could find a job practicing law there with no problem or even hang out my own shingle."

"What about your wife?"

"I would do anything to get away from that hellion," he said. I started to agree with him, but figured I should keep my opinions to myself.

"You still haven't told me why you are in Dallas," I said.

"Looking for Jill," he said. "I started at the last place she worked."

"And what did you learn?"

"They haven't seen her," he said desperately. "No one has seen her since last Monday."

"And what are you going to do?"

"Keep looking," he said.

I got out of the car and left him there with his head down. He seemed a defeated man. I had a feeling that his problems were just beginning.

Chapter 17

Things were beginning to make more sense to me now. It was logical for a man obsessed with a woman— a woman he would do anything for—to buy a radio station in another town just for her. Smitten men have done much more than that. It was also logical for a woman obsessed with a man to manipulate another man to get herself into position to manipulate the man she wanted. And if such was the case, what went wrong? Where was the woman? The better answer was that she and the other male had run away together. The easiest way to answer that question was to simply wait until Lamar Crafton was supposed to return from Alaska. If he didn't show up, then it was a matter of tracking down the runaway couple, a fairly easy task given enough time and money. But what if Crafton showed up and Polaris was still gone? Several precious days would have been wasted in the wait.

As the 727 made its final approach into Memphis International Airport, I listed things to do: (1) check airport parking lot; (2) have frank interview with Kadley Sturgis; (3) interview Ellie to find out where she and Jill were going Tuesday morning (Why did Ellie lie to me about Jill?) and (4) re-interview Veronica Crafton. Tomorrow would be a busy day. I also needed another payment from Kadley Sturgis. His retainer fee had already been eaten up by expenses. If I calculated my earnings based on time I had spent on this case so far, I would be working for less than minimum wage.

After arriving in Memphis, I made my way through the concourse and directly to the parking lot, stopping only to make a call to the Heritage House to let Deborah Taylor, the innkeeper, know that I was returning tonight. Unfortunately for me, she was booked up tonight and suggested that I call Rebecca Fentress, owner of the Oak Grove, another bed and breakfast in the area. I did so and was told that the cottage was available. When I told her that I would be arriving in two hours, she said that she would meet me "on the front porch."

The thought occurred to me that my Crown Victoria rental car might have met the same fate as the Firebird in Dallas. As I approached the area, my pace slowed and I scanned the lot. It was not yet night, but dusk had already cast its filtered, reflected light on Memphis. I stole a glance over my shoulder, then stepped out to the section of the parking lot where the car was left yesterday.

The Crown Vic was still there, just like I left it. I visualized a car bomb exploding. The thought took me back to a time twenty years earlier when one of my police officer colleagues paid fifty cents to a young ghetto kid to start his car every morning during an undercover investigation in the bowels of St. Louis. When I asked my friend how he would feel if the car exploded with a kid in it, he replied simply that "at least

I would be alive to have some sympathy for him."

I opened the door, got in, held my breath and turned the ignition key. The car started. I waited for thirty seconds. No bombs went off. I exhaled. I backed out of the parking space and drove across the lot to the section where Crafton's Jeep had been parked. It was still there, bumper sticker and all.

Chapter 18

The Oak Grove Bed and Breakfast was located on Highway 178 in Union County, a few miles outside the city limits of New Albany. Unlike the Heritage House, a large city home, the Oak Grove was a cottage. Built in 1907 as an addition to a pre-Civil War log home, it was rescued from demolition in 1994 by a woman who wanted to save it. The cottage was moved from its original site to its current location, restored and modernized with central heat and air-conditioning.

The small cottage takes its name from the nearby Oak Grove cemetery and church. One of its more interesting features is an elaborate, white, cast iron bed, which purportedly belonged to a lady of the night in Texas. She supposedly had it custom made. It is so heavy that reinforcing supports were added under the floor. The head and foot boards were adorned with carved birds and hanging grapes.

I pulled up in the driveway and parked beside a ten-year-old dark sedan. It was hard to make out the year and type of car because darkness was now complete. As I got out of my vehicle, a woman appeared on the front porch and walked to the top of the steps. She was in her late fifties, maybe early sixties. The lines of her face were deep, especially the crows feet around her eyes. Nevertheless, the clothes she wore—gray pants, a white blouse and pink sweater—made her look stylish and younger. Her hair was salt and pepper, still mostly pepper. No sign of hair coloring, although it was difficult to tell in the night light. If she were a car, I would have to say that the body was in decent shape, but that there was excess mileage.

"You must be Mr. Boulder," she said in a sweet southern accent. When I answered in the affirmative, she said, "I'm Rebecca Fentress. I manage the property for the owner. Come on inside and let me show you the place, then I'll leave you alone. This is not exactly a motel room, so I need to get you acquainted with the facilities."

We walked into the sitting room of the cottage through double doors with wavy glass panels. Several shaded lamps cast a warm light on antique furnishings

and Victorian lace curtains. From the fireplace came the warm glow and coziness of gas logs. All it would take now is rain on the tin roof and I would have to be extricated from this place. No wonder I had grown such a distaste for motel rooms.

There were two large windows on one wall. Both rose from the floor to a height of about six feet up the wall. In front of one window was a loveseat; in front of the other, a matching chair. A small drop-leaf table opposite the loveseat was covered with white linen cloth and a china place setting for two. Rebecca walked to the other side of the room and pointed out a sink, a counter with a toaster, and a microwave. Opposite the counter was a small bathroom decorated in dark red, complete with a ball and claw foot bathtub. The sitting room opened to the bedroom and the madam's bed.

"And that's the fifty-cent tour," she announced, handing me a business card with her name and telephone number printed in red on it. I followed her to the front porch. "I live nearby, so call if you need anything. By the way, how long will you be staying?"

"Possibly just one night," I answered.

"You're the private detective, aren't you?"

"I'm a private detective," I acknowledged softly.

"Looking into Jill Polaris' disappearance, right?"

"That's right," I said.

"I think that a woman did it," she said, crossing her arms and lifting her chin.

"Did what?"

"Who knows what?" she said. "Got rid of her. Whatever they did."

"Why do you say that?"

"She was a threat. A threat to another woman," she said, inching over to the front steps. She began walking down the steps sideways with her right hand on the rail.

"Wait," I insisted. "What woman?"

She walked slowly to her car, head downward. She opened the driver's door, then looked back at me and said, "Veronica and Ellie. Who else?" before driving off into the night.

I stepped back into the cottage. I knew what she meant about Veronica, but what was Ellie's involvement in this? Going straight to the source seemed like the best idea. I picked up the telephone, called the Heritage House and asked to speak to Ellie Saline. She was on the line about a minute later answering with a bubbly hello.

"Ellie," I said cautiously. "This is Jack Boulder. I need to talk to you."

"No, you don't," she said. "There is nothing to talk about."

"I don't want to talk about us," I said. "I want to talk about Jill Polaris and you."

"What do you mean?"

"I would like to talk to you face-to-face, if that's okay."

"Come on over if it's that important," she said.

I drove directly to the Heritage House. She was waiting in the living room. It was now almost nine o'clock p.m. When I beheld her, a strange feeling went through me. Gosh, she was beautiful. I sat on a sofa. She chose a chair.

"So what is this about?" she asked.

"Ellie, you told me that the last time you saw Jill was Monday night. You were seen leaving here with her in her car Tuesday morning. What do you say to that?"

"I lied," she pronounced with a smile.

The sound of footsteps making their way up the front steps and across the porch could be heard. We turned our heads to the front door. Through the screen I could see a man. With a smile, he spoke a greeting to Ellie.

"I've got to go," she said. "My date is here."

She got up and bounced to the front door. As she opened it, she turned to me and said, "Meet me here at five o'clock tomorrow morning. You will understand then," she said to my puzzled look.

I sat there awash in a mixture of feelings, as she and the man, who looked fifteen years younger than me, walked down the steps and drove away in a new Camaro.

Chapter 19

After a fitful night's sleep in the madam's bed at Oak Grove, I got up at 4:30 a.m., showered, shaved, dressed, and made the short drive back to Heritage House in the predawn darkness. The morning air was cool, so I added a light jacket to my usual wardrobe of khakis and polo shirt.

Ellie was waiting in the living room, which was almost dark except for the light from a small lamp on the mantle. As I drove up, she came outside and joined me in my car. She wore blue jeans and a windbreaker with the words "New Albany Bulldogs" on the front.

"Let's go for a ride," she said.

"Where to?"

She gave me directions, and after a few turns, told me to pull to the curb in front of a house up ahead on the right. I looked at her curiously and she gave me a "don't worry, silly man" look. We got out of the car and walked toward the house. The aroma of fresh-baked cookies or cakes filled the morning air. Ellie knocked on the door. Inside I heard the scuffling of feet. The door opened and a woman in her early to mid-seventies stood behind the screen door. She recognized Ellie immediately.

"Can we interrupt you a minute, Mrs. West?" said Ellie. "I want you to meet somebody."

"Why, it would be a pleasure to be interrupted by

you, my dear girl," said the lady. "Please come in."

She headed toward the back of the house. "Why don't we go back to the kitchen? We can talk while I finish boxing up the cakes."

We entered a kitchen where pots and pans laced with sugar and flour and all kinds of baking ingredients were laid out on counters. On one counter were several large white boxes with plastic see-through windows.

Mrs. West excused herself and went into her bedroom. I took the opportunity to attempt to find out what Ellie was up to.

"Ellie, what is going on?" I whispered.

"Would you think Mrs. West and her cakes are a good human interest story?"

"The best," I said. "She ought to get an award from the governor or something. But what does this have to do with Jill Polaris?"

"This is where Jill and I went on the morning she disappeared. She wanted to do human interest stories on unique people in New Albany. Mrs. West was the first. As you can see, one must be here pretty early in the morning to get the full story."

"Who else was she going to do stories on?"

Just then Mrs. West entered the room. "Are you talking about that nice radio lady?"

"Yes," said Ellie. "I was telling Jack here about her feature stories."

"I told her about two interesting people," said Mrs.

West, opening her oven. "One is the luckiest man in New Albany and the other is Alfred. Those are two of the most interesting men I have ever met." She continued to work while she was talking. "The luckiest man in New Albany was ordained by his mother to be that way."

"How so?" I asked.

"In Mississippi, black-eyed peas will bring luck. But only if eaten on New Year's Day. The traditional New Year's Day lunch is black-eyed peas, hog jowl, turnip greens and corn bread. One of our more colorful ladies here in New Albany decided that she wanted her grandson to have lots of luck. So on New Year's Day, she did more than just give the six-month old child some black-eyed peas. She dipped that baby in a big pot of them. Now, far be it from me to say whether it worked or not, but that boy has been successful in spite of himself. He is now a prominent downtown businessman."

"What about the guy named Alfred?" asked Ellie.

"Well, Alfred is a real piece of work," Mrs. West replied as she continued her task of preparing cakes. "Most people around here think of him as kind of the local town drunk. And while it is true that he tends to stay a little inebriated from time to time, he is a good person. He has even been known to check himself into jail when he has had a little too much to drink. Anyway, not long ago he found two hundred dollars that somebody had lost downtown, and he marched straight to the police department with it. When I heard about that incident, I took him a cake right away."

"What kind of cakes are these?" I asked.

"Cream cheese," she replied. "It takes about two hours to bake a cake, so I get up early, do my baking, then go back to bed. I got the recipe from a lady at the bank. I baked a cake for one person, then another and before long it seemed that everybody in town wanted me to bake them a cake."

"Mrs. West, we need to get going," said Ellie. "I just wanted you to verify that Jill Polaris came by to see you."

"She did indeed. And a nice girl, I might add."

We graciously left the home of Mrs. West. When we got back in the car, Ellie turned to me and said, "There's one thing I didn't say in there, but it was what Jill was interested in most."

"What's that?" I asked.

"Mrs. West gives all the money from her cake sales to the church for the youth."

"Good for her," I said, hoping not to sound sarcastic.

"Over the years, she has contributed over $60,000 to her church from those cream cheese cakes."

Now I felt like a heel. So Jill Polaris was out researching good news stories. That was a twist. Ellie told me that she had walked back to the Heritage House that morning. She said Jill was headed straight for work, as far as she knew. It was time to pay another visit to Kadley Sturgis. However, it was still early, so Ellie and I took in breakfast at Jimbo's.

Chapter 20

"How was your trip to Memphis?" asked Sturgis.

There was something about him that was different from before. He seemed pretty nervous, but it was more than that. His body language was talking loudly. He put his hand to his chin and I noticed it. His fingernails were gnawed to the skin, the redness standing out like he had dipped his fingers in light red oil. I would have noticed such a condition on my previous visits with him. This was something new. Here was a nervous man indeed.

"It was fine," I said. "But I did not stop with Memphis. I also went to Dallas."

The news settled on him like a spray mist, saturating him slowly. His eyes looked down to his lap.

"And?"

"And I found out a little more about Jill Polaris. I also found out a little more about Kadley Sturgis. You have quite a reputation as a sales agent, Mr. Sturgis."

"Who told you that?" he asked, his head remaining down.

"Your former colleagues at the radio station," I said.

Looking up at me he said, "How much do I owe you, Mr. Boulder?" He reached in his desk drawer and pulled out a checkbook and opened it.

"I don't know, exactly," I said. "I need to figure my expenses."

"Go ahead and give me a number we can settle on," he said, putting pen to check. "Make it a little high if you like. I want to settle our account now, and I want you to go back to Jackson."

I could have probably told him any number and he would have paid it, but extortion is illegal. He was clearly a man who was very desperate and who wanted me out of New Albany. Was I reading his desperation wrong? Could it be that he was being threatened? Was there someone else here? He had all the earmarks of a man pushed to the limit.

"Why don't you just pay me what you think my work was worth," I said. "If it's too low, I'll tell you."

"Fair enough," he said, scribbling rapidly on the check. When he was done he tore it from the checkbook and handed it to me. It was for three times what my highest bill would have been. "Can we consider our account settled?"

"We can," I said.

"Goodbye, Jack Boulder."

I got up and walked out of his cold gray office. He remained seated at the desk. By now it was after five o'clock p.m. and the receptionist had already gone.

Kadley Sturgis did not walk me to the door and that was fine by me. He was one client that I was happy to be done with. As I walked through the reception room, I had another idea. I opened the heavy metal front door and closed it, staying inside the reception room. I tiptoed to a storage room off the reception area and squatted down behind a file cabinet. I strained to hear Sturgis. Within a minute I heard a door open in a room that was behind the wall that I was leaning against. I focused my hearing on the other side of the wall. I thought I heard water running, and realized immediately that on the other side of the wall was the restroom. Sturgis was relieving himself.

I got up and walked quickly, but quietly, back through the reception room to a door that led to a back hallway. I opened the door with a minimum of sound and scooted into the back hallway, where I discovered four metal doors, each of which had a four-by-four inch viewing hole with wire-reinforced security glass. The door on the back wall obviously led outside, another door led to another hallway, the third provided access to a small office, and the fourth was to the stairwell. I chose the last one. I wanted to see what was upstairs.

The door was heavier than the others, but I managed to open it without any disturbance to Sturgis. He was probably finished with his break and back at his desk. Presumably he would then be leaving. The stairway to the second floor was narrow. It had one turn and then yet another metal door at the top of the stairs. I opened it a little faster and encountered a hallway of jail cells on my right. I could hear the hum of radio and electronic equipment coming from that direction. Directly in front of me was another short hallway with a barred window at its far end. Its light showed me what I had been hired to find. Sitting in a metal folding chair, gagged and bound, was none other than Jill Polaris.

Chapter 21

Her hands were tied behind her back with what appeared to be ski rope. A four-inch piece of dark green duct tape was over her mouth. Her feet were bare and unbound. Around her neck was a white ski rope tied in an executioner's noose. The rope led from her neck up and over a curved rod in the ceiling and down to a metal lever that came up from the floor. Under her chair was a set of drop panels, the kind used in hangings. I think it's called a drop door.

Jill's eyes were dark and sunken. If she had been here since the day she was reported missing, she would be weak indeed. Her eyes looked at me with curiosity, rather than hope. She did not know if she were about to be rescued or punished. It appeared that she had suffered here. Her left eye was black. She wore blue jeans and a thick gray tee shirt, the kind that football teams practice in. From the looks and smell of her, my guess is that she had been here the whole time.

I decided it would be best to thoroughly check out the ski rope rig before I did something foolish. Sure enough, it was set up so that if Jill attempted to move more than an inch or so, the rope would trip the lever, which would in turn open the drop door. Jill Polaris would fall straight down through the ceiling of the first floor. Her neck would break and she would die almost instantly.

Further inspection revealed that the rope setup was only designed to keep Jill in place. If I untied the rope or cut it, all that would happen would be that the rope would simply slacken. I looked into Jill's eyes as if seeking guidance. She looked responsive, but dazed. I walked over directly in front of her and reached out to her face to remove the duct tape from her mouth. As I did so I heard the squeaking sound of an opening door at the bottom of the stairs. I put my finger to my lips and signaled a "shhhh" to Jill. She nodded in agreement. I could see in her eyes that she was coming to life.

I turned and headed for the row of cells where the radio equipment was placed. As I moved in that direction, I could hear footsteps coming up the stairs. All of the cell doors were open and various radio equipment was set up in each cell. The equipment was bulky and placed dead center in each of the six cells. Most of it was about six feet high. I picked the second cell, moved in, and hid behind the equipment as best I could. I heard the top door open and then the voice of Kadley Sturgis.

"So, how is my Jill doing today?" he said in a mocking voice. "Have you reconsidered my offer?" There was a long pause. "Why don't you think about it one more night? Then tomorrow I am going to do what I am going to do with you." Another long pause. "You are so very beautiful, you know."

Then I heard the sound of a slap. Probably across her

face. It was all I could do to restrain myself from simply charging out and grabbing him. It would be a pleasure to break his arm and give him a swollen kidney while attempting to restrain him. But I knew better. All he would have to do is give a slight tug on the ski rope and Jill Polaris would fall through the floor. I remained still, my heart pounding in my ears. Waiting. What was he doing now?

From the cell beside me, I heard the slide and the thud of the cell door closing. I heard the steps and then the slide-thud-clang of my cell door closing. This continued for four more times and I realized that he had closed all of the cell doors. Was I trapped until morning? All I could do was wait and listen to his footsteps as he walked back down the cell row, open the door to the stairway and then leave.

I silently cursed myself. Instead of rescuing Jill Polaris, I was now in captivity as much as she. I listened as hard as I could and thought I heard the front door of the building open and close. Kadley Sturgis was probably gone for the night and here I was stuck with a piece of radio equipment as a companion for the evening. Wait a minute! The radio station stayed on twenty-four hours a day. The evening program was simply a feed from some network over a telephone line that was rebroadcast from the station's transmitter. If the equipment in my cell could somehow disrupt that signal, it would probably mean that the station would go off the air. Sturgis would probably know about it and come back down to the station to repair it. There was probably a plug I could pull or a switch I could flip on this equipment in the cell with me. I walked around the equipment inspecting it as if I knew what I was doing. All I knew was that it was humming, that there were a few small lights on it and that there were wires and fuses on the back of it. Just for the heck of it, I reached out and pushed sideways on the cell door. It slid open with just a little effort!

To say I felt foolish would be an understatement. But I did not have time to dwell on my shortcomings. I walked out of the cell and back down the hall to Jill Polaris. The left side of her face was red and splotchy. I removed the duct tape from her mouth.

"It's going to be all right," I said. "I'm a private investigator hired to find you. Just hang on and I'll get you out of here."

Behind me the door at the top of the stairs suddenly opened and Kadley Sturgis stood there with a .38 Chief's Special in his hand. It was pointed at my face.

"I'm afraid that is not going to happen, Mr. Boulder."

Chapter 22

Kadley Sturgis took three steps forward and, still pointing the gun at me, said, "Move over to the window."

I did as he ordered, given that I did not have much choice. He took three more steps forward and now stood in front of Jill.

"Have you ever been to an execution, Jack Boulder?" he said.

"Yes," I lied.

"Good," he said, taking a step backward. "You can assist in this one. Come over here, please. I would like for you to be the executioner."

"What do you mean?" I asked.

"Jill Polaris is about to be executed for her crimes," he replied. "I will administer last rites, then you will conduct the execution. It's very simple. All you have to do is pull that lever."

"No, Kadley, no!" pleaded Jill.

He took one step forward and slapped her across the face. I made a move forward, but he was much faster that I calculated. He pointed the gun at me before I could get close to him.

"Forget it, Boulder," he said. "Put the tape back over the prisoner's mouth."

I did as he said. The look in his eyes was that of a crazy man. Anything could happen. All I could do was try to buy some time.

"Your move to New Albany did not turn out to be what you thought it would be, did it?" I intoned.

"Shut up," he said.

"Which was worse, Sturgis—finding out that she had an old flame, or realizing that you could never make her love you?"

"I told you to shut up," he said waving the gun.

"One more question then," I said. "How much did it cost to give me that little warning in Dallas?"

"Are you kidding?" he said with a laugh that sounded like Santa Claus. "That cost me nothing. I have many friends who owe me a lot in Dallas. Now shut up and get over here while I pronounce the sentence. Put your hands on that lever."

I moved over to a position beside the lever. Jill began squirming slightly. Sturgis spread his feet apart in the manner of a pastor. He pointed the gun directly between Jill's eyes.

"Jill Polaris, you have been convicted of the unpardonable crime of fraudulently misrepresenting your love, and further for causing . . ."

His speech was interrupted by a rattling of some kind. It sounded as if it was in the direction of the front door. It grew louder. Sturgis cocked his head and listened closer.

"What the hell is that?" he said angrily. I had to think fast.

"It's the police, Kadley," I said seriously. "You don't

think I would have stayed here without calling out the cavalry, do you?"

He was confused, attempting to figure out if I were bluffing. It did not matter. The important thing was that someone was at the front door banging away.

"Stay here," he commanded, turning sideways and walking to the door of metal bars. He opened it, then slammed it shut. "Don't try to go anywhere. You are locked in now," he said, descending the stairs.

When his head disappeared down the stairway, I reached over and pulled the noose from around Jill's neck. She hopped off the drop door and struggled to the corner of the hallway by the front window. She withered to the floor and assumed the fetal position. It would be a long time before she recovered from this ordeal. There was no telling what Sturgis had been doing to her. I put my ear to the small window, just above the front door. I could hear a voice yelling to be let in, and pounding on the front door. Then I heard the front door open and the voice of Sturgis.

"What do you want?" he asked.

"It's time for me to come in." It was the drunken voice of Alfred, the man who had asked me if I wanted to hear his song. He was trying to check into jail. Just like the town drunk in that old TV comedy.

"Get out of here, you idiot," yelled Sturgis. "The jail is over that way."

The front door slammed shut. I knew what was

going to happen now unless I took immediate action. Sturgis would come up the steps and either shoot both of us or make us hang each other. There was no way out. Or was there?

I scooted over to the drop door and stood directly in the center of it. Reaching over for the rope, I grabbed it and yanked it as hard as I could. The other end of the rope jerked the lever from its position, opening the drop door. I fell straight down into the first floor hallway. As I hit the floor I saw Sturgis to my right. He reeled backward and I saw shock in his blood-covered face. The heavy metal drop door had sprung open at precisely the instant he was about to walk under it. It caught him right in the face. He fell to the floor in a heap like a prize fighter who had just been knocked out with a vicious right. I opened the front door and there was Alfred standing at a soldier's sloppy attention stance as if waiting his turn to come in. He looked down at the sight of Sturgis on the floor and the growing pool of blood around the radio station owner's head. He turned and stared at me with a curious look, then passed out, corkscrewing himself onto the front steps. I grabbed a telephone and called the police, requesting them to send an ambulance as well. I dug into the pockets of Kadley Sturgis in search of the key to the jail door at the top of the stairs. I had no success. What the heck. It was better for the police to handle all of this anyway. I was about ready to join Alfred in la-la land.

The New Albany police arrived literally in less than one minute. The ambulance soon followed. I gave Sgt. Perkins the short version of what had happened. We could do the long version tomorrow morning.

Chapter 23

The next morning I woke up sleepy. The events of the night before had left me physically and mentally exhausted. Now, lying here in the madam's bed at the Oak Grove Bed and Breakfast, all I wanted to do was turn over and go back to sleep. But sleep would not come. Neither would alertness. I was in a mental fog, neither asleep nor awake.

Mechanically, I got out of bed and pulled back the curtain on the window. The morning light was unexpectedly soft. Perhaps it was cloudy and about to rain. What time was it anyway? I stepped back to the nightstand beside the bed and sought out my wristwatch. It informed me that it was six twenty-two a.m. No wonder it was not bright with sunlight outside. The sun was just now making its ascent. It had been a long time since I had been in the country in the early morning. My mental fog was beginning to clear. I slipped on a pair of khakis and a shirt and walked over the threshold of the cottage's front door and onto its porch. I sat in one of the rocking chairs and surveyed the scene. Here I was—a barefoot, front row audience member looking at a theater set created by God. The air was still and moist. Patches of fog hugged the treetops across the field before me. On my left, about fifty yards away, a white-tailed deer emerged from the woods and grazed at the edge of a meadow. The rat-a-tat-tat of a woodpecker was heard some undeterminable distance behind me. In the side yard two blue-jays squawked at each other in aggressive conversation.

I just sat there, rocked slowly back and forth, and took it all in. If there was another human being within ten miles, there was no evidence of it. No highway noise, no slamming doors, and no lawn mowers. To my right, I noticed a hawk perched vigilantly atop a telephone pole scanning the field below for a sign of movement in the ankle-high grass. Suddenly it dove off the pole, down onto the ground. It appeared that the bird had intentionally crashed awkwardly into the weeds and grass. Its movements were nothing like the beauty of the golden eagle, which, with razor-like talons, snatches its prey in a graceful downward arch. Three seconds later, the hawk was airborne and flying away. In its claws was a small field mouse that would soon become food for its predator.

The more I observed this scene of nature, the more obvious it became that it was not as peaceful as it appeared. The deer, which had paid no attention to the hawk, would return to the woods and spend the day in silent survival. The birds would search for food and be on constant alert. Things are seldom as they first seem. Enough philosophizing. It was now seven-thirty a.m. Time for me to go to the hospital.

Chapter 24

Jill Polaris was in Room 408, according to the receptionist. A quick elevator ride, a walk down the corridor to the right, and I was quietly opening her wide hospital door. She lay asleep in the bed, which was elevated slightly so that she was partially sitting up. Sitting beside her was Ellie, reading a paperback novel. Ellie gave me a sympathetic smile and stood up.

"She won't be awake until about noon," said Ellie softly, looking down at the swollen, bruised face of Jill. "They have her under sedation so that she can rest."

"Will she be in the hospital a long time?" I asked.

"The doctor doesn't think so. She has been hit in the face a few times. Otherwise, there is no sign of physical injury. Emotionally—they don't know yet."

"What do you think she will do?" I asked.

"About staying in New Albany?"

"Yes. I guess that is what I meant," I said.

"That's her decision," said Ellie. "But I have made my own decision."

"What is that?"

"I am going to move back to New Albany," she said pensively. "In my line of work, I can relocate anywhere. It might as well be at a place close to my heart. Besides, the people here don't seem to mind outsiders. I feel welcome here. I talked with a lady at that downtown development organization yesterday. She told me about a space on the second floor of a building on Bankhead Street. There is a possibility I could remodel part of it into an apartment and use the rest of it as a great big office."

"That sounds like a fine idea," I said.

"Do you need to talk to Jill when she wakes up?"

"Perhaps later. But not today," I said. "Are you going to stay with her?"

"Yes."

There was nothing left to be said. "See you later, Ellie."

"Good-bye, Jack," she said, sitting back down. Damn, she was good-looking.

Chapter 25

Kadley Sturgis was to be arraigned at two o'clock p.m. I had assured Sgt. Perkins of the New Albany Police Department that I would come in this morning and give him my formal statement. It was now time to keep that promise. I drove back downtown, parked on West Bankhead across from City Hall and walked the short half-block to the police department. Sergeant Perkins was waiting for me. With a combination of the efficiency of a big league law enforcement agency and the friendliness of a small town police officer, he took my statement, tape recorder on the table between us, and note pad in his hand.

He was primarily interested in the events at the radio station and not the aspects of my investigation. He did not ask about my trip to Dallas and I did not volunteer any details about it. As far as I knew, Lamar Crafton had not committed a crime, and it was not my place to instigate speculation about his activities.

After an hour and a half, Sergeant Perkins had all he needed. I assured him that I would be available if there was a trial. I bid him farewell and walked out onto West Bankhead Street, the doors of the police department closing behind me.

For me, this case was now over. My mission had been accomplished. I had found the girl. I had been paid. My client, however, had committed the crime and gotten arrested. I couldn't help wondering: Why did he hire me in the first place? The obvious speculation would be that he wanted a cover for what he was doing with Jill. In his mind, he probably thought that he could convince her to love him. When she did not respond accordingly, he was trapped. His mind was sick, and I would wager a dollar to a doughnut that his future was at the state hospital for the criminally insane instead of the state penitentiary.

Back at my car I decided I was not quite ready to leave New Albany just yet. I needed to walk up and down the two blocks of a real, small-town downtown with its mildly-congested traffic and pedestrian-lined sidewalks. When I got to Sappington's, I looked in the window at the clothing racks and decided I needed a new pair of khakis and a couple of polo shirts. Most men don't buy new clothes, they merely replace old ones. A friendly, enthusiastic store owner took care of my needs. He was so friendly that I bought an extra half dozen polo shirts.

As I paid the bill, I said, "This is your lucky day."

"Every day is my lucky day," he replied. "I'm the luckiest man in New Albany."

He sent me on out with a smile on my face. I walked on past a bookstore, the Village Café, scene of the Crafton incident, and a hardware store. As I passed an alley on my left, I had the sense that someone was walking a little too close behind me. I stopped suddenly, and a hand was on my shoulder as a man bumped into me on my right side.

"Hey man. Want to hear my song?"

It was Alfred. The same Alfred who had tried to get into jail the night before. The same Alfred who walks the streets of New Albany in his own little world of make-believe. The same Alfred who saved my life.

"I would love to hear your song," I said with a grin.

"Listen. They are playing it on the radio right now," he said, taking off the greasy headset and handing it to me. I put the earphones over my head and pretended I was listening to the best music that I had ever heard. I even snapped my fingers to an imaginary beat.

"Man, that is a good song," I said.

I handed the earphones back to him and he replaced them on his head. I considered giving him some money, but I knew that if I did that, he would just find a way to buy some cheap wine. I had another idea.

"Alfred, let me see that radio on your belt," I said.

He complied without a question and tagged along behind me to the inside of a variety store. I found the most expensive radio and tape player combination to replace the one he thought he listened to and then purchased it, a cassette tape of the greatest hits of the eighties, and a set of batteries. Back outside, I placed the tape in the player, put it on his belt and placed the earphones on his ears. Then I turned it on. His eyes opened wide and a big grin came upon his face. He turned around and walked down the street, waving his hands in the air as if conducting a symphony orchestra.

My day was now complete.

I went back to my car, pulled out and drove around the block past the courthouse and the radio station before heading back onto West Bankhead Street. As I crossed the Tallahatchie River, I left downtown New Albany in my rearview mirror and drove to Jackson without stopping. Most of the way my mind was in that alpha state of self-hypnosis as I replayed the events of the past few days and their implications on everyone concerned. The last thirty miles of the trip seemed to never end. I wanted to see Laura in the worst kind of way.

Finally arriving in the capital city at four o'clock p.m., I returned the big Crown Victoria to the car rental agency and then got behind the steering wheel of my 1968 Camaro. The car was covered with the film of neglect that an automobile gets when it is not driven and taken care of. Its familiar interior did not alter my mood as much as I had anticipated. I drove to my reserved space at Capitol Place, my downtown condominium complex, entered my private domain, and immediately placed a telephone call to Laura, whose secretary told me that she was in a meeting but would call me back shortly.

The little light on the answering machine blinked a beckoning bright red at me. I picked up a yellow legal pad and pen and noted the messages one-by-one. Most were routine or inconsequential. Except the last one, which had been left at three fifteen this afternoon, according to the computer-generated, female-sounding voice from inside the machine.

"Mr. Boulder, I need you to call me the moment you receive this message." I vaguely recognized the voice, but could not place it. "Please consider this an urgent matter. This is Lamar Crafton."

He then gave a local telephone number that I immediately recognized. It was the switchboard at Laura's law firm. I replayed the message several times. His voice was a combination of business and urgency. I had no clue what I was about to face.

Chapter 26

I walked out of my condo, across tree-shaded Smith Park and into the lobby of Deposit Guaranty Plaza, the twenty-story downtown office building that houses a variety of upscale tenants, including Laura's law firm. It was almost five o'clock p.m. and many downtown workers were beginning to make their way to their cars, which would take them to their suburban homes. Not many of us live downtown these days. Some were no doubt leaving early to go to college football games that would be played tomorrow in stadiums around the country.

I stood in front of a bank of six elevator doors and waited what I thought was a little too long for the "up" arrow to illuminate simultaneously with the ding of a bell. The chrome middle door opened and the elevator disgorged its human contents in my direction. I stepped back and let the people walk purposefully past. Once inside the elevator, I stood alone and mashed the button for the floor on which the receptionist for Laura's law firm was located. Her gang of legal eagles took up two or three floors—I could not remember which—of the top part of the building. The elevator door opened into a foyer of rich, wood paneling, with molding shaped in the form of columns such as those found on the front of federal courthouses. It was all very formal, very impressive and very unfamiliar because it was my first time to set foot inside this place. I opened a heavy wooden door and was greeted by a receptionist who looked hurried, like she had a small child waiting for her at a day care facility.

"I'm Jack Boulder," I said. "Here to see Lamar Crafton."

Standing up, she said, "Yes, Mr. Boulder. He is expecting you. Please come this way." She led me to a small interior conference room and asked if I wanted anything to drink as she showed me a seat. I declined and she left me alone in the windowless room, leaving me to speculate on the value of windowed and corner offices. Two minutes later Lamar Crafton walked in. He was dressed in a dark blue, pin-striped suit, white shirt and yellow necktie. He looked more comfortable in this environment. Thanking me for coming, he said, "I want to talk to you about doing something for me."

With that comment I had about all I wanted of Lamar Crafton. He was a self-centered lawyer, husband, and man, as far as I was concerned. I did not like his brand of ambulance-chasing or the way he planned to run away from his wife. He was running either way. It was time he stayed in one place and accepted his responsibilities. On the other hand, I was not very impressed with his wife, either. I was on the verge of telling him where he could take his request. But I kept cool, being the professional that I am. I would hear him out.

"And what might that be?" I asked.

He sat across the table from me and said, "You are the only person in Mississippi who knows that I went to Dallas."

"So?"

"I would be most grateful if you would keep that to yourself. It is very important to me."

"Are you planning to return to New Albany next week and pretend that you went on a hunting trip to Alaska?"

"That's right," he said.

"Your personal life is your business, Mr. Crafton," I said. "But allow me to ask you a few questions if I might. I would like to understand the situation a little more."

"Go right ahead," he said.

"For starters, what are you going to tell Jill?"

"First, let me explain a few things," he said solemnly, leaning forward. "When Jill Polaris came to New Albany, I was on top of the world. You probably do not know this, but we went to college together. We were in love. I wanted to marry her, but she did not want the life of a small town lawyer's wife. She went off in search of her career and I went back to New Albany after law school. I was young, concerned about social justice and never really got over Jill."

"How did Veronica come into the picture?" I asked.

He continued as if he had not heard my question. "Most of my clients were poor people. Some needed help getting their social security check or their veteran's benefits. Some were people charged with crimes and had no lawyer to represent them. My work was extremely self-satisfying, but I wasn't making much money. My law partner seemed to tolerate it, but I wanted to contribute more to the firm—financially." He paused a minute, as if reflecting on his legal career, then looked me in the eye.

"Veronica?"

"Yes. You asked about Veronica. I have known her all my life. In retrospect, obviously what she wanted was a small town, rich lawyer to indulge her dream of becoming a famous interior designer. I let her push me into changing into a plaintiff's attorney, one that went after insurance settlements. I guess it worked. Within six months I was rolling in dough. She was ecstatic. She even asked me to marry her. You should have seen the wedding."

"I hate to interrupt your life story, Mr. Crafton," I said. "But my question was regarding your going back to New Albany next week. Or perhaps you are going to New York and wait on Jill Polaris?"

"You have a right to ask," he said. "I have decided to go back to New Albany next week. I have not been a very good lawyer, or a very good husband, for that matter. I want to be the kind of lawyer that my father was. Someone who was concerned about the law and about justice. My father was also a good husband.

Something I have not done very well. I am going to stay with Veronica and try to be a better husband."

"What are you going to tell Jill?"

"Jill and Veronica want the same thing—fame and fortune for themselves," he said. "In Dallas I realized how much fame meant to Jill. So both women want the same thing. I want something else. But, you see, I am already married to one of those women. Leaving her and going to the other will not help me find what I am looking for."

"And what might that be?" I asked.

"Respect. The same kind of respect my father had."

Lamar Crafton's words sounded good. But he was all mixed up. He did not know what he wanted. I think all he knew was that whatever he needed to make his life meaningful would be found in New Albany. Another person had come to the same realization within the past few days. All Ellie needed was New Albany. It was time to tell Lamar Crafton what he wanted to hear, and let him get on with his life without having to worry whether a man named Andrew Jackson Boulder would reveal his secret.

"Mr. Crafton," I said, "as far as I'm concerned, I never saw you in Dallas. Don't worry about me. Go take care of yourself."

"Thank you."

"One other thing. If I ever need a good lawyer in New Albany, will you be available?"

"You bet I will."

"One more thing," I said. "What is your connection to this law firm?"

"We affiliate with them from time to time. They do work for us in Jackson and we do work for them in north Mississippi. Do you work with anyone from this firm?"

"Yes," I said. "You might say that I am acquainted with one of their partners."

We shook hands and I left him standing in the conference room. I walked out and saw Laura down the hall. She looked at me in surprise.

She came to me and said. "Well, isn't this a pleasant surprise? Welcome back."

"Thanks," I said. "I just met with Lamar Crafton, a lawyer from New Albany. How much longer are you going to be here?"

"Five minutes," she said. "Our meeting just broke up."

"How about we find a place for a romantic dinner and I will tell you all about my New Albany case?"

Chapter 27

It was Saturday morning, and Laura and I were driving north back toward Oxford for the Ole Miss Rebels' second home game in a row. This week's game did not have the pressure associated with it that the Ohio State game had the week before. Nevertheless, Laura was excited. I had told her all about the case—conveniently omitting the Ellie part. Laura seemed to have a real soft spot for Jill and was annoyed with me for not checking on her. The evening before, we had a long discussion about it. Laura said that the case was unresolved.

"No," I had told her. "The case is resolved. It's the story that is not complete."

She wanted to know what had happened to Jill and whether Lamar actually came back to town and pretended he had been to Alaska. I wanted to know, too. But it was not my place to find out. My work was done.

It was another beautiful Saturday. The sun was bright and another hint of autumn was in the air. The Jaguar was purring like a kitten as we rode up Interstate 55.

The cellular telephone in Laura's car rang. She picked it up and answered with her name. I hoped we did not have to go back to Jackson on unexpected law firm business.

"It's for you," she said, handing me the telephone. I thought I detected a grin. Was this a practical joke?

"Hello," I answered cautiously.

"Hello, Jack Boulder. This is Jill Polaris and you are live on New Albany radio on a special Saturday morning edition of the Jill Polaris show." At regular intervals I could hear a beep.

"Uh, good morning," was all I could say.

"Jack, you and I have never formally met, but I wanted to call you on the air and say thanks to you for what you did. I am deeply grateful."

"Thank you."

"By the way, are you enjoying the trip up to the big game this morning?" she asked. That is when I realized that someone had put her up to this telephone call. Someone sitting beside me, as a matter of fact. I was smiling inside all of a sudden.

"I'm enjoying it immensely, Jill. But it's a little better since I heard your voice. How are things in New Albany?"

"Things in New Albany are great as always, Jack. Reconciliations have taken place and things are getting back to normal," she said. I took that as a code that Mr. and Mrs. Crafton were back together.

"And how is Ms. Polaris?" I asked.

"Jill Polaris is wonderful, Jack. But she will be moving on from New Albany to the bright lights of New York."

"My congratulations," I said.

"Thank you for all you did, Jack," she said. Music

began playing in the background. "Well, I can tell by the sound of the music that another hour has come to an end, so it's time for me to wrap it up. This is my last hour on the air in New Albany. I thank all of you who have supported me, and I promise that I will not forget you." The music grew louder. "From New Albany, Mississippi, this is Jill Polaris saying that I hope all your days are good ones. Remember—every day is a special day. Thank God for it."

The music in my ear continued for a few seconds, there was a click, and then Jill Polaris was gone.